# ICE CREAM QUEEN

# ICE CREAM

# QUEEN

Coco Simon

Simon Spotlight

New York   London   Toronto   Sydney   New Delhi

This book is a work of fiction. Any references to historical events, real people, or real places are used fictitiously. Other names, characters, places, and events are products of the author's imagination, and any resemblance to actual events or places or persons, living or dead, is entirely coincidental.

SIMON SPOTLIGHT
An imprint of Simon & Schuster Children's Publishing Division
1230 Avenue of the Americas, New York, New York 10020
This Simon Spotlight edition August 2020
Copyright © 2020 by Simon & Schuster, Inc.
All rights reserved, including the right of reproduction in whole or in part in any form.
SIMON SPOTLIGHT and colophon are registered trademarks of Simon & Schuster, Inc.
For information about special discounts for bulk purchases, please contact
Simon & Schuster Special Sales at 1-866-506-1949 or business@simonandschuster.com.
Text by Tracey West
Jacket illustrations by Alisa Coburn
Designed by Hannah Frece
The text of this book was set in Bembo Std.
Manufactured in the United States of America 0720 OFF
10 9 8 7 6 5 4 3 2 1
ISBN 978-1-5344-7117-7 (hc)
ISBN 978-1-5344-7116-0 (pbk)
ISBN 978-1-5344-7118-4 (eBook)
Library of Congress Control Number: 2020939778

# CHAPTER ONE
## SLAYING IT!

"Tamiko, you're going to be late for your first day of school!" Mom yelled up the stairs.

"COMING!" I yelled back. Mom was being unreasonable. I still had ten minutes to get to the bus stop, and I needed to upload my blog post before I left.

I'd just taken a mirror selfie of me in my back-to-school outfit: baggy ripped jeans and a white T-shirt with cartoony bright orange carrots on it. I started typing.

"And here's the winning outfit! Thanks for voting in my poll yesterday. I brought home so many cool outfits from Tokyo that I couldn't pick one.

"Now I'm off to start another year of school. The

good news is that I finally have a class with my bestie, Sienna! 😍😍"

"Sienna" was the code name I used on my blog for one of my best friends, Sierra. My other bestie, Allie, was code-named "Anne" because her favorite book was *Anne of Green Gables*.

I started to type, "The other good news is that I don't have to take art this year with Mr. Rivera. I love art, but that class bored me to tears!" But I deleted it after just a few words. Before the summer had started, I'd gotten into some big trouble for posting something negative on my blog that I'd meant to be funny. So I was trying to be really careful about not posting anything hurtful.

Instead I typed: "If you're going back to school today too, remember to be your fabulous self, walk tall, and don't let the haters get you down! That's Tamiko's Take."

I studied the selfie, making sure I was okay with the image. My face was covered up by a huge bunny emoji. I knew I was following basic online privacy rules, but I had to admit that the emoji made me look a little silly. Oh well.

I quickly checked over the text for typos, and

then, with a satisfied sigh, I uploaded the post.

"TAMIKO!"

I tucked my phone into my backpack, slung the bag over my shoulder, and bounded down the stairs and into the kitchen. Dad was seated at the kitchen table, calmly drinking a cup of coffee.

"Why is everything so loud this morning?" he asked.

"Yeah, why?" parroted my older brother, Kai, who was halfway out the front door. Outside I could see a blue car parked in front of our house.

"Who's that? Are you getting a ride? Can I get one too?" I asked.

"That's Kevin, who's a senior, and no," Kai said.

"But—" I protested.

Kai closed the door behind him, and Mom ran up to me and handed me a lunch bag and a granola bar.

"You need to get to that bus stop, Tamiko," she said. "I'm bummed that you didn't come downstairs earlier. I made the pancakes and everything."

I glanced over at the stove, where pancakes that looked like smiling frog faces were stacked on a plate. Mom had gotten a pancake mold when I was four years old, and she'd made me frog pancakes on special occasions ever since—and always on the first day of school.

"Save them and I'll microwave them tomorrow," I said.

"You're *welcome*, Tamiko," Mom said. Then she looked me up and down. "This is the outfit that your blog readers picked?"

I did a twirl. "Yup!"

Mom sighed. "I voted for the white shirt with the black jumper. It looked so cute on you."

"My readers have spoken!" I said. "Bye-eee!"

I raced out the door and jogged down to the corner bus stop. Even though it was September, the temperature still felt summery, and I was glad to be wearing the T-shirt today. When the bus came, I found a seat, tuned out the noise and the smell of middle school BO, and took out my phone. First I checked my blog. Three comments already! Then I texted Allie.

Have a great first day of school! Bet you can't wait to see Colin!

She texted back: You too! Bet you can't wait to see Ewan!

I groaned. Served me right for teasing her about

Colin. I replied with a tongue-stuck-out emoji and leaned back in my seat.

Last year I'd had art class with Ewan Kim, and he was nice, and funny, and definitely the best thing about that class. And during the summer when I'd been in Tokyo, he had texted me almost every day, sending me pictures of stuff in Bayville so I wouldn't feel homesick. And now I was kind of confused. I liked talking to him and wanted to hang out with him more, but I was pretty sure I didn't have a crush on him. At the same time, I couldn't help but wonder if maybe Ewan liked *me*. It was hard not to think about it when Allie and Sierra were constantly teasing me about him!

Allie texted back with another tongue-stuck-out emoji. I locked my phone and stared at my lock screen—me and Grandpa Sato with our heads together, smiling into the camera. I'd had a blast in Tokyo, just like I did every summer. My dad had been born there, and Grandpa Sato still lived there, so we visited him every year.

This year had been extra fun because I'd been on special assignment for Molly's Ice Cream shop, which was owned by Allie's mom, Mrs. Shear. Sierra,

Allie, and I worked there on Sundays, and I handled social media for the shop on the side. Mrs. Shear had given me fifty bucks to try as many flavors as I could of Japanese soft cream, which was basically like soft-serve ice cream here in the States. They had so many cool flavors in Japan. I'd tried black sesame, soybean flour, and even miso-flavored soft cream. (Yes, the same miso that's in miso soup.) Everything was really delicious. I couldn't wait to see if Mrs. S. was going to come up with any new flavors based on my research.

The soft cream posts had been a big hit on my blog too, but given how well my blog was going, I thought I could post pictures of paint drying and that would be a big hit. That's why they called me the queen of social media! And by "they," I meant me and sometimes my friends, but I was confident that more people were going to get the hang of calling me that soon.

The school bus came to a stop, and I walked out into a scene of pandemonium. Everybody was super-excited to see one another after the summer. I spotted Sierra and our friend MacKenzie and ran up to them.

"Yay, carrot shirt!" MacKenzie said. "I voted for that one."

"Well, I voted for the purple-and-red minidress," Sierra said. "But you look adorable in this, too."

"Thanks!" I replied, and then I eyed Sierra's look, a pleated gray-and-black skirt that fell to just above her knees, and a short-sleeved red sweater. Her thick, curly hair was pulled back with a black headband. "You look fabulous, Si. I need to do a blog post about fall fashion with you."

Then I looked at MacKenzie, comfortable in skinny jeans and a green T-shirt with a rainbow across the front.

"You could join too, Kenz," I offered.

MacKenzie laughed. "No thanks, Tamiko. I'm not into fashion like you two are."

"One of these days," I said, and then we made our way into the building.

I dropped my lunch in my locker and then headed to my first class, Spanish. As I made my way through the halls, I got stopped by a few kids, most of them complimenting my outfit.

"I read every single blog post you put out this summer," my classmate Kyra told me. "Tokyo looks like an amazing city. I hope I can go there someday."

"It's a long plane trip, but totally worth it," I told her with a huge grin.

It was really cool to know that I still had so many blog readers. I mean, I always got a count of who was reading my posts, but to get feedback in person felt great—kind of like I was a celebrity!

Finally I got to Spanish class, and there stood Ewan! He smiled as soon as he saw me.

"Hey, it's the world traveler," he said.

"Hey, it's the guy who was stuck in Bayville all summer," I replied.

Ewan laughed. "It wasn't so bad. You know, people come from hours away to spend the summer in Bayville. The beach is great."

"This is true," I agreed. "Hey, let me see your schedule."

Ewan showed it to me, and I frowned.

"This is the only class we have together!" he said.

"Really? That's disappointing," I said. "But hey, look on the bright side! At least we—"

*"Hola, estudiantes!"*

A woman with short, black hair walked into the room.

"*Me llamo Señora Hernandez*," she said. "In this class we will be seated alphabetically. So *escúchame, por favor*. I will call out your names. Leesa Allan, please take your seat here in the front row. . . ."

I looked at Ewan and frowned. "You're a *K*, and I'm an *S*, so . . ."

"See you at lunch, I guess," he said.

Señora Hernandez had a lot of energy, and class was very intense, in my opinion, for the first day of school. She even gave us homework!

The rest of my day went pretty smoothly and uneventfully. That was a little disappointing, actually, because I was hoping for something exciting that I could write about in my blog. "Food fight in the cafeteria! Teacher who wears crazy ties! Gym class confessions!" But everyone behaved themselves at lunchtime, we didn't even suit up for gym, and only one of my teachers wore a tie: Mr. Miller, my third-period English teacher, and his was a very tasteful navy tie with black pinstripes. Nothing to blog about there.

The highlight of my day was science class with Sierra, my last class of the day. The teacher was a guy about my dad's age, with dark black hair and a cool-looking mustache.

"I'm Mr. Olabarietta, but everyone calls me 'Mr. O.,'" he began. "Please take a seat where you feel comfortable."

I looked at Sierra and beamed. We could sit together! Some boys got the best seats in the back row, but we found two seats next to each other right in the middle of class.

"We've got a lot of exciting topics coming up this year," Mr. O. continued, "but I'd like to begin the first day of school by getting to know you. Please introduce yourselves by name and tell me what your animal mascot is."

"What if we don't have a pet?" somebody asked.

Mr. O. shook his head. "No, I mean an animal that you relate to, that you feel shares some of your personality traits," he explained. "For example, my animal mascot is a cheetah, because I like to run. Now, who wants to go first?"

There was an awkward moment as just about everybody stared down at their desk, hoping they wouldn't be called—including me. I could be outgoing at times, and I liked getting attention on my blog, but Allie had recently explained to me that I was what is known as an ambivert—someone who is partly introverted and partly extroverted. The introverted part of me could spend hours and even days happily by myself, creating things. And sometimes I could get shy.

Sierra, however, was a true extrovert, and she raised her hand.

"My name is Sierra Perez, and my animal mascot is a cat—not a big cat, like a cheetah, but a house cat," she said.

"And why is that?" Mr. O. asked.

"I have a cat named Marshmallow, and she's so curious and excited about everything," Sierra said. "And that's just like me!"

You know how they say that a person's smile lights up a room? That was Sierra. She beamed when she was talking about her cat, charming everybody. It was like this special magic that she had.

The extrovert in me wanted to get in on some of that magic, so I raised my hand.

"My name is Tamiko Sato, and my animal mascot is also a cat," I said.

"Why?" Mr. O. asked. "Do you also have an adorable cat at home?"

"No. It's because I rule over my house, I never

obey commands, and I love treats," I said, and everyone in class laughed—including Mr. O. I'd nailed it!

"Well, I did not expect that," he said, wiping his eyes. "I think we've found our class clown."

"I'm not a class clown," I replied. "I have a much better fashion sense than that. But you can call me 'class queen.'"

"Hmm. I think there's only room in this class for one monarch, and that's me," Mr. O. teased. "Okay, who wants to follow that?"

I smiled. I liked my classes, I liked my teachers, and everyone thought I was funny. A thought popped up in my head.

*I can feel it. This year is going to be the Year of Tamiko!*

## CHAPTER TWO
# CHANNELING MY CREATIVITY

I caught up with Sierra in the hallway after class.

"How'd the rest of your day go?" I asked.

"Not bad," she replied. "But I have Mr. Rivera for art. Now I know what you were complaining about all last year. The way he described the projects we'd be working on almost put me to sleep!"

I nodded. "It's not easy. But if I could get through it, you will!"

Sierra sighed. "Other than that, I got a ton of homework assigned. Can you believe that? Who gives homework on the first day of school?"

"You are not alone," I told her. "I've got a ton to do when I get home."

"Then it's a good thing you finished your submission

for the *Bayville Monthly* magazine cover contest," Sierra said.

I stopped. "Wait, what?" I asked. "I thought that was next week?"

Sierra looked at her phone. "Nope. You've got to get the digital file in by midnight tonight. You asked me to put an alert in my phone because you said you wouldn't remember. Remember?"

I hugged her. "What would I do without you?" I asked. "When I become a famous fashion executive, will you be my personal secretary?"

"Hmm, Tamiko, that's not exactly the dream career I imagined," Sierra replied.

"Well, anyway, thank you!" I said. "I am a genius for asking you to remind me."

"Or am I a genius for knowing how to use a basic calendar app?" Sierra asked, in what I thought might have been a teensy dig, but I couldn't tell from the tone of her voice. It was ironic, actually, because Sierra was usually the one who was too busy and couldn't keep track of her schedule.

Anyway, I couldn't stick around to find out if Sierra was teasing me or not.

"See you tomorrow, Sierra!" I said, and I ran to

catch my bus, still imagining myself as a famous fashion executive. I liked the image!

When I got home, I let myself in with my key because there was no sign of Kai yet, and I knew that Mom and Dad didn't get back from their work at the college until six on Mondays. Luckily, they'd decided that I was old enough to stay home by myself for a few hours.

I rushed up to my room to finish the art submission that Sierra had reminded me about. I dumped my backpack onto my bed and headed into the little side room attached to my bedroom. We lived in an old house, and Mom had said the little room might have been some kind of baby nursery when the house was built. But with lots of windows letting in bright light, it made the perfect space for me to do my creative work.

Some people might have called it a craft room, but I preferred to call it a DIY room, because I was not making macaroni picture frames like some kind of summer camper. I was creating and customizing things—like, I'd turn a torn pair of jeans into a cute denim purse, or decoupage a lampshade with pages from manga to decorate my room with.

The room was turquoise with white trim, and all my tools and materials were stored in jars and plastic bins. My main workspace was a big metal folding table that I'd picked up from the curb. It held my grandma's vintage sewing machine and still had room for me to create.

Right now the table was covered with stuff I was using for my art submission. *Bayville Monthly* was a magazine that talked about all the things to do and places to go in our little beach town. When tourists came to visit, they used the magazine as a guidebook, and any businesses that were featured in it usually got more traffic.

Every year *Bayville Monthly* held the Bayville County Youth Arts Contest, where they invited artists up to age eighteen to submit art about their favorite thing about Bayville. I figured that a lot of people would be submitting photos or drawing pictures of typical stuff, like ocean waves or the boardwalk. But lately I'd been having fun making collages, and as the (unofficial) social media director of Molly's Ice Cream, I knew how amazing it would be to get the ice cream shop on the cover. Free publicity!

So I'd started making a Molly's Ice Cream—

themed collage. First I'd printed out some of my favorite photos of Molly's: the vintage metal letters that spelled out ICE CREAM that hung on the wall, a jar of rainbow sprinkles, Allie's little brother eating an ice cream cone. Then I'd collected paper stuff from the shop, like a napkin with the shop logo, and one of the paper menus that we kept by the register. I'd arranged everything on a piece of cardstock, and then to fill in the gaps I'd searched through my supplies to find some fun additions. A scrap of fabric with rainbow-colored polka dots reminded me of the sprinkles, glitter cardstock added some sparkle, and cutout pictures of ice cream from some kiddie magazines from Japan looked really cute.

When I made collages, sometimes I just put the images together, and *Bam!* I was done. But I'd agonized over this piece, moving things around again and again. Now I had to finish it.

I picked up my glue stick, took a deep breath, and attached the first image to the cardstock. I kept going, tweaking my arrangement as I went, and using liquid glue for the fabric. When I was done, I stepped back and held it up.

"Cute," I said. "But it needs something."

Then I spied some glittery pom-poms in one of my bins.

*Perfect!* I thought. They'll give it some dimension! But I didn't want to go overboard, so I carefully plucked out a few black ones and some white ones, to match the ice cream shop's black-and-white checkerboard floor.

When I glued on the last pom-pom, I grinned. The whole thing just looked right. Next I placed the image in a special photo box I'd made with a white bottom and walls, which I used to photograph stuff for my blog. It helped me get a clean, perfect image without any weird shadows.

I took a few pictures on my phone, chose the best one, and then went to the magazine's website. I filled out the online form and uploaded the photo with the caption: I ♥ Molly's!

Then I texted the image to Allie and Sierra. What do you think? 7 hours before the deadline!

Allie replied first. I love this! I'm going to show it to my mom as soon as she gets home!

I texted her back. Tx. How was your first day at the luxury spa known as Vista Green?

I was teasing Allie about her school. She, Sierra,

and I had all gone to the same elementary school together, which was how we'd become besties. But then Allie's parents had divorced, and Allie had moved to a different part of Bayville with her mom. That's why Allie went to Vista Green School instead of MLK with Sierra and me. Vista Green had just gotten remodeled a few years ago, so everyone around town knew that Vista Green had much better school equipment and cafeteria food than we did. I thought it bugged Allie when we teased her about it, but sometimes I couldn't resist.

LOL! she replied. It's been a good day so far. Lots of classes with my friends. ☺

You mean your OTHER friends, I teased. Seriously, tho, that's nice. Homework?

Nope, she replied. We had getting-to-know-you games all day, and pizza.

☺🔊!!!! I typed back. No work, no homework, and pizza on top of it! It was hard not to be jealous of the Vista Greenies sometimes.

Sierra chimed in. Your cover looks great, Tamiko!

I was typing a response to her when I heard the front door open.

"Tamiko, we're home!" Mom yelled up the stairs.

"Come on down and tell us about how your first day of school went."

I went downstairs to meet them. Dad was behind Mom, carrying two pizza boxes with white bags piled on top, and Kai was walking in the door after them.

"Where've you been?" I asked. "Business club meeting?"

"What else?" Kai asked, and he walked past me without another word.

"Since it's a special day, Dad and I picked up dinner from Calabria's," Mom announced. "Can you two please set the table?"

"Yay, pizza!" I cheered.

I ran into the kitchen, where Kai was pouring himself a glass of water from the pitcher in the fridge.

"Mom wants us to set the table," I said.

"What's stopping you?" Kai asked.

"Wow, looks like somebody ordered their pizza with a slice of attitude," I said, surprised. As big brothers went, Kai was a really good one. He never teased me or bugged me, and he was generally a chill person. Chill emotionally, I mean. When it came to schoolwork and his goals, he was on fire. He wanted to be a billionaire businessman someday.

I was hungry, so I grabbed plates from the cabinet and napkins from the drawer and didn't argue with Kai. Soon the four of us were seated around the kitchen table, and Dad opened the pizza boxes. I inhaled the steam that came out of them.

"Half plain for Kai, half pepperoni for me, half olive and anchovy for your mom, and half veggie for Tamiko," Dad said.

That might sound like a lot of pizza, and it was—we always had leftovers. But we Satos were very picky about our pizza and could never agree on just one kind to share. So this had been our family pizza order for at least the last two years.

"Now tell me about school," Mom said, and I chatted away about how Sierra and I had one class together, and what a big hit my outfit was, and how I had cracked everyone up in Mr. O.'s class.

"And Allie didn't even have regular classes or homework today!" I went on. "And they had pizza! And I was having pizza envy until you walked in the door, and now I'm not."

I turned to Kai. "Did you get a ton of homework too?"

Kai shrugged. "It's school. There's homework. What did you expect, Tamiko? A band playing live music and balloons?"

I rolled my eyes. "Well, I didn't expect a ton of homework on the very first day, that's for sure."

"And how much of that homework have you started?" Mom asked.

I shifted in my seat. "Well, none, actually. I had to finish this art project for—"

Dad shook his head. "You know the rule, Tamiko. Homework first, then fun."

"Do we have to send you back to the after-school program?" Mom asked.

"No!" I said quickly. "I'll do my homework right after pizza, I promise."

Mom squinted at me, like she did when she was trying to make a point. "And the rule?"

"Homework first, then fun," I promised.

Then things got quiet as we ate our pizza. *Stupid rule,* I thought. *Rules kill creativity!* I imagined living on my own when I grew up and making my own rules, and I smiled. Then I sighed. That was such a long time to wait!

Kai got up from the table before anybody else and

left without being excused. When he got upstairs, I looked at my parents.

"What's up with him?" I asked.

Mom shrugged. "He's probably exhausted. The first day of school can do that to you."

I frowned. I'd just had *my* first day of school, and *I* wasn't snappy or exhausted. Also, Kai regularly could spend all day at school, run in a track meet, and then come up with a business plan for his club without even yawning.

What was up with my big brother?

## CHAPTER THREE
# FABULOUS FALL FLAVORS

Beads of sweat poured down my back as I ran along the concrete trail. Up ahead, I could see the bouncing ponytail of one of my teammates. I quickly glanced behind me and didn't see anyone, but the path had curved.

It was the first cross-country meet of the season. I wasn't really into playing sports, and neither was Kai, but Grandpa Sato had said he didn't want his grand-children getting lazy, so we'd both started running to prove him wrong. Kai liked running as fast as he could, so he'd joined the track team. I was more of a slow and steady runner, so I'd joined cross-country.

Some cross-country teams were intense, but I liked how low-key it was at my school. You showed up, you ran, you went home. I wasn't terrible, and I wasn't great. I usually finished the two miles in about seventeen minutes, which was pretty average for girls on my team. I had never placed higher than fifteenth in a meet, but that had never bothered me. I was running to be healthy and prove to Grandpa Sato that I wasn't lazy.

The muscles in my legs were starting to burn, and as I turned another corner, I was glad to see the finish line in sight, flanked by the coaches and a few parents. When I crossed the line, Coach Furman yelled out, "Sixteen minutes and forty-two seconds. Great job, Tamiko!"

I grabbed my water bottle and took a sip. "Really? That's my best time."

"And you're in ninth place out of forty girls," Coach Furman said. "I knew you had it in you."

Coach Furman was a young guy with a crew cut, the kind of person who liked to use motivational sayings. He told me to *dig deep*, and he said things like, *I'll never give up on you; you can only give up on yourself!* This was the first time I'd gotten an *I knew you had it in you* from him. And then I realized something else.

"Ninth place," I repeated. That was in the top ten!

"Keep pushing yourself, Tamiko," Coach Furman said, "and you'll go far."

I was so excited that I video-chatted with Grandpa Sato as soon as I got home, and told him the news.

"Very good, Tamiko," he said. "I knew you had it in you."

I laughed.

"What is so funny?" he asked.

"You sound like my coach," I told him.

"Then you have a very good coach," Grandpa Sato said.

While I was talking to Grandpa Sato, Kai walked into the kitchen.

"Kai, I placed ninth in my cross-country meet today!" I told him.

To my surprise, Kai didn't say *anything* in response. He just took a bag of crackers out of the cabinet and walked away.

"Was that your brother?" Grandpa asked me.

"I'm not sure," I replied. "I think an alien has taken over his body. He's not acting like the Kai I know."

"We all have times when we do not feel like ourselves," Grandpa Sato said. "If you are worried about him, why not just ask him?"

"I should," I said, and I meant to, after I got off the video chat with our grandpa. But Kai holed himself up in his room for the rest of the day, and he was still asleep when Mom drove me to Molly's Ice Cream shop the next morning.

"Bring home a pint of the Coffee Caramel Chip, please," Mom said, shoving cash into my hand as I got out of the car. "I can't stop thinking about it."

"Are you sure you don't want one of our new fall flavors?" I asked her. "We're featuring them today."

"Coffee. Caramel. Chip," Mom said, very slowly. "Please."

"Got it, Ayumi," I replied, because it bugged Mom when I called her by her first name, and then I made a quick getaway into the shop.

I usually arrived about fifteen minutes early to take photos or get ideas from Mrs. S. for the Sunday social media post that would bring customers into the store. That was just before the lunch rush. Today I found Sierra already there, filling napkin dispensers, and Allie was writing on the small chalkboard next to the ice cream counter.

"You're an early bird today, Si," I said.

"Don't be so surprised," Sierra replied. "I just

27

wanted to get some extra Allie time in. I miss her now that school's started."

"Well, I miss her too," I said, and I walked over to Allie. "New quote? Or an ice cream pairing?"

Allie wrote a column for her school paper where she paired books with ice cream flavors, and she had started writing pairings on the board in the shop as well, or literary quotes about food. The customers seemed to like it.

"Pairing," Allie replied, without turning back to look at me. "Almost finished."

Seconds later she stepped back from the board. She'd written:

*Today's Pairing*

*Read: The Cow Loves Cookies*
*by Karma Wilson*

*Eat: Vanilla Cookie Dough Ice Cream*

She'd even drawn a cute little cow.

"That's adorable, Allie," I said.

She grinned. "Thanks! I brought in my copy of

the book from home, so if a kid actually wants to read it, they can."

She propped the book up on top of the counter.

"Brilliant!" I said, and I took out my phone. "I need to do a post about the new fall flavors. I was thinking, 'Come on down to Molly's for our Fall Flavor Fiesta,' but I don't think 'fiesta' is quite right. That makes it sound like we're actually throwing a party."

"How about 'It's always a party at Molly's!'" Sierra suggested. "We always have fun, don't we?"

"That's true, but we don't want customers to show up and be disappointed," I said. "Mrs. S. said to promote the Pumpkin Caramel Swirl, Maple Butter Pecan, and Apple Pie flavors. I need a word that sounds more fall-like."

I turned to Allie. "What about 'Come on down to Molly's for our Fall Flavor Extravaganza'?"

"I kind of miss the *F* alliteration," Allie said. "How about, 'Come on down to Molly's for our fabulous fall flavors'?"

"What about 'festive'?" Sierra asked. "Festive fall flavors."

I ran through the possibilities. "Fierce fall flavors?

Finest fall flavors? Fresh fall flavors? Fattening fall flavors?"

Allie gasped. "Don't you dare!"

"Just kidding, Ali-li," I said. "I like 'fabulous.' I'm going with that."

I typed out the post, being sure to mention the shop's hours and the featured fabulous fall flavors. Then I took photos of the ice cream to add to the post.

Sierra glanced outside. "There are some people still wearing shorts. It doesn't feel like fall."

"If we waited for it to feel like fall, we'd miss out on the whole fall-flavor trend," Allie said. "Mom researched it, and customers expect fall flavors in stores right after Labor Day."

"If fall flavors are what they want, fall flavors are what we'll give them!" I vowed.

Then the little bells on the door chimed as our first customers arrived. Since we'd started working together, the Sprinkle Squad, as we called ourselves (as well as the Sprinkle Sundays sisters), had divided up the tasks. I took the orders. Allie made the orders with an assist from me, and Sierra took the payments and made the change.

Two teenage girls walked up to the counter.

"Welcome to Molly's! Would you like to try one of our fabulous fall flavors?" I asked in a cheerful voice.

The girls were not in a fabulous fall mood, because they ordered chocolate milkshakes, and I didn't try to change their minds, like I sometimes liked to do. They looked happy with their order.

"I finished in the top ten at my cross-country meet yesterday," I announced to Allie and Sierra when the girls had left.

"Tamiko, that's awesome!" Sierra said.

"Congratulations!" Allie added.

"Well, you know, Coach Furman said he always knew I had it in me," I said. "Just another thing to add to the list of things I'm good at."

I caught Sierra raising her eyebrows at Allie.

"What's wrong with me saying that?" I asked. "We're all multitalented. Allie, you're an amazing writer and reader and you help your mom run the shop. Sierra, you're a great singer and athlete and you're super-friendly. What's wrong with being proud of your talents?"

"There's nothing wrong with that," Allie said.

"Just maybe there's a difference between being proud and, you know . . ."

"Bragging," Sierra finished. "Bragging is so uncool. Like those people who brag on social media all the time about their new clothes, and the fancy trips they go on, and—"

"You mean like when I went to Tokyo?" I asked, feeling defensive.

"No! I mean, that was different, because you have a blog, and you're just letting your friends know what's going on in your life," Sierra said, brushing a strand of curly hair away from her face. "I didn't mean you, *chica*, honestly."

I still had the feeling that Sierra and Allie thought I was bragging all the time, but I didn't get a chance to ask them because more customers came in, and time moved quickly. I talked up the fall flavors, which was easy. A *lot* of people wanted our Pumpkin Caramel Swirl ice cream. After the first hour Allie's mom came in from the back freezer with a new tub of it.

"You girls must be doing a great job pushing the new flavors," she said. She had the same dark brown hair as Allie, and she held it back with a bandana printed with ice cream cones.

"I think the social media post is bringing them in, Mrs. S.," I said, and right after she headed into the back room, a man and a woman stepped up to the counter.

"You're right," the woman told me. "As soon as I saw online that you had Pumpkin Caramel Swirl ice cream, I made a beeline here. I love pumpkin ice cream!"

"And pumpkin spices, and pumpkin cookies, and pumpkin candles," the man teased her. "I'm surprised you didn't marry a pumpkin instead of me!"

"Are you a pumpkin hater?" I asked him.

"Pretty much," he replied. "I mean, I've eaten pumpkin pie, but all the pumpkin stuff out there is just . . ." He made a face.

"Molly's flavors are all-natural, so our Pumpkin Caramel Swirl ice cream is nothing like the sugary artificial flavor that you might find in other stores," I said. Then I smiled at him. "I can make you a special sundae that will convert you one hundred percent into a pumpkin lover!"

The man looked at his wife. "What do you think, Nilsa?"

"Do it, Michael!" she said. "I'll take the same sundae too."

Michael nodded at me. "I accept your challenge!"

I thought quickly about what flavors might go well with pumpkin. I wasn't too worried, because I knew Mrs. S.'s ice cream would probably be enough to convince him on its own. But I wanted to wow this pumpkin hater.

"Two scoops of pumpkin in a sundae dish, Allie," I said. "Times two."

Allie, who'd heard the whole exchange, was giving me that *What are you up to now?* look, but she didn't like to argue in front of customers. I took the ice cream from her and topped it with a dash of cinnamon, a generous helping of candied ginger, and a swirl of chocolate sauce. Before I handed them their sundaes, I topped them with chocolate sprinkles.

"Here's your sprinkle of happy!" I said, pushing the sundaes forward on the counter.

"Oh my goodness, this looks delicious!" Nilsa said.

"We will see," Michael said in a skeptical tone.

He took a bite right in front of me, and I watched his face carefully. He didn't say a word or change his expression, but he took another bite. Then he looked at me and smiled.

"The sweet creaminess of the pumpkin is well balanced by the spicy ginger, and the chocolate adds extra depth," he said. "I've never tasted anything like this before. I love it!"

"Welcome to the pumpkin family!" his wife teased him, and she turned to me. "I've been trying to get him to like pumpkin for as long as we've been married. It's a miracle! Thank you!"

"Just doing my bit for the pumpkin lovers of the world," I said.

They moved down the counter and paid, and then sat down. Sierra ran over to me.

"That was so cool," she whispered. "How did you know that the pumpkin and ginger would work together? Have you had it before?"

"It was just a guess," I admitted. "It sounded good in my head, so I went for it."

Allie was behind us. "That was risky," she said. "What if he didn't like it? He might have refused to pay for it."

I shrugged. "Well, he loved it, so relax, Ali-li!" I said.

Allie frowned, but she went back to her station as more customers came in. I knew she had a point. It was risky to serve something that you haven't tasted. But I was feeling really confident about everything in general. School and cross-country were going great. I was still the queen of social media.

Why couldn't I be the ice cream queen, too?

## CHAPTER FOUR
# 100 PERCENT AWESOME

"Blue skies and sunshine are great, but I'm waiting for a fall chill in the air so I can break out my favorite fall fashion items: cardigans and boots! Here's a sneak peek at some of my faves that I'll be breaking out when the temps drop. If you had to give up wearing cardigans or boots for the rest of your life, what would you choose? Comment below!"

I scrolled through the comments on my blog on the bus ride to school. It was a few weeks into the semester, and I still hadn't convinced Kai to let me ride with him and his friend to school.

The blog comments were overwhelmingly in favor of keeping the boots and ditching the cardigans, but I think if I had to choose to keep one or the other forever, I'd pick cardigans. I think they look cute on me, and they're an easy way to change an outfit from something casual to more polished.

I hadn't meant for *Tamiko's Take* to be mostly about fashion, but people seemed to like when I posted pictures of clothes or modeled outfits. Even though I did a lot of fashion posts, I also liked doing posts about food, and stuff that happened at school. That was a nice way to mix things up, I thought.

I read the most recent comment.

"Love your blog, Tamiko. You have such an artistic eye! You are so creative!"

I realized that I didn't recognize the commenter's name. *My blog must be getting popular,* I thought. *Why wouldn't it? It's awesome!*

I was in a great mood when I arrived in Spanish class. Ewan smiled and waved at me, but Señora Hernandez walked in before we could talk.

"*Buenos días, estudiantes,*" she greeted us.

"*Buenos días, Señora Hernandez,*" we all replied in unison.

"Before we continue with our lessons today, I'd like to give you a short quiz to see how everyone is doing so far," she said. "This way I can tailor our lessons to everyone's abilities, and we can find ways to support one another."

She started passing out the quiz papers while some of my classmates exchanged nervous looks. I picked up my pen and dove right in. The questions were mostly fill-in-the-blank, but at the end we had to write a few lines about something we were wearing or something we'd eaten that day. I looked down at my black jeans, white button-down shirt, and black flats.

*Estoy llevando jeans negros y una camisa blanca con botones. Mis zapatos son . . .*
For extra credit I added a line about my red necklace.
*. . . zapatos bajos. Mi collar es rojo.*

I looked over my work, and then Señora Hernandez said our time was up.

"While I'm grading these, I want you to write a description of an animal you know. Write about how that animal looks, and what it does," she announced.

There were a few groans as we pulled out our notebooks. I didn't have any pets, so I wrote about my Grandma Sasaki's cat, Sora. I was trying to think of the Spanish word for "peach," because that's what color she was, when Señora Hernandez cleared her throat.

"You all did fantastic, class," she said. "And we even had one perfect paper. *Felicidades*, Tamiko!"

The other kids burst into applause, and Ewan gave me a thumbs-up from across the room.

"*Gracias*," I said, and I felt really proud and happy.

"Some of the material on this quiz will also be on our first big test of the semester next week," Señora Hernandez continued. "We'll be reviewing it all week, though, so don't worry if you found the quiz challenging."

*No problem for me,* I thought. *I'll ace the test, just like the quiz!*

Sierra had a club meeting during lunch, so MacKenzie and I sat together and picked at our mixed vegetable stir-fry, which honestly looked like it had come from another planet.

I texted Allie a picture of the lunch and added a caption: Guess what you're NOT missing at MLK!

That looks so gross! Allie replied. Then she sent a picture of her own school lunch. We have a fall harvest bowl today.

I sighed when I saw the colorful bowl of sweet

potatoes, apples, greens, and grains. Everything looked so fresh and appetizing.

"Hey!" MacKenzie exclaimed. I looked up from my phone, and she pointed at my lunch with her fork.

I examined my plate and gasped. One of the carrots in my stir-fry was shaped differently from the rest—and it looked just like a heart!

"Wow," I said. "Who knew something so adorable could exist in an MLK lunch?" I snapped a photo of the heart-shaped carrot with my phone. This was definitely going up on my blog later that day.

"It must be a sign of good luck!" MacKenzie said, taking a photo with her phone too.

MacKenzie must have been correct about the lucky omen, because I had another great moment in science class with Mr. O. We were starting a unit on atoms and molecules.

"Which subatomic particle is charged with negative energy?" he asked.

A joke popped into my head, and I raised my hand.

"Um, my mom and dad before they have their coffee in the morning?" I asked.

Mr. O. cracked up, and I got a rush.

"Nice guess, Tamiko, but I'm looking for sub-atomic particles, and I'm guessing your parents are about my size," he said.

"Just kidding," I said. "The answer is electrons."

He got a twinkle in his eye. "Are you positive?"

"If I were positive, I'd be a proton," I shot back, and he laughed again. I looked over at Sierra, who was shaking her head and laughing.

At the end of class a bunch of kids walked up to me. I was a little startled.

"You're too funny, Tamiko," Victoria said.

"Yeah, you could be a stand-up comic," added Ryan.

"I'm not *that* funny," I said, but I was just pretending to be modest. I knew I could probably be a great stand-up comic someday, if I wanted to.

Sierra and I left the room together. "Wow, it's like everyone knows you," she said.

"That's how I feel about *you*," I told her. "You're the rock star, remember?"

We made our way to our lockers, and as we passed the school office, the secretary, Ms. Shipman, stepped out. She had a huge grin on her face.

"Tamiko, glad I caught you," she said. "We just got a special delivery to the school that you need to see."

I gave Sierra a puzzled look, and she followed me inside. Ms. Shipman walked to a pile of magazines on the counter.

"*Bayville Monthly* dropped these off, because they thought we'd want to see what one of our students had achieved," she said. "The issue will be on stands next Wednesday."

She handed me a magazine. There, on the cover, was my Molly's Ice Cream collage!

Sierra let out a squeal. "Oh my goodness, *chica*, you did it!"

I read aloud the blurb on the cover. "'Winner of the Bayville County Youth Arts Contest: Tamiko Sato, a student at MLK Middle School.'" Then I began to jump up and down. "I did it! They picked my art!"

A bunch of kids who had come into the office to see what the commotion was about started to clap and cheer. Even Principal Harrison came out of his office to congratulate me.

"Well done, Tamiko," he said. "We're very proud of you for winning."

"Of course I won!" I blurted out. "I'm naturally talented!"

Sierra laughed. "Congratulations, my sassy, confident artist friend!"

Ms. Shipman handed me three more magazines. "Take these home to your family. Now, don't be late for your bus, superstar!"

"Thanks!" I said, beaming.

As soon as I got onto my bus, I called Allie on video chat. I held up the magazine in front of the camera.

"I won the *Bayville Monthly* contest!" I told her.

"Wow, congratulations!" Allie cheered. "My mom is going to be thrilled."

"Tell her to start making more ice cream," I said. "Business is going to explode!"

Allie laughed. "I sure hope so!"

We ended the call, and I gazed out the bus window, musing. It felt great to win the contest—really great! In fact, it was like *everything* was going well for me recently. I was totally winning at life!

Why should I stop at being queen of social media or ice cream queen? Why not be queen of *everything*?

## CHAPTER FIVE
# KAI'S SECRET

I waited until Mom and Dad got home to tell them the great news.

As soon as I heard the front door open, I ran down the stairs with a copy of *Bayville Monthly* in my hand. Mom and Dad were both thrilled, of course.

"This calls for a celebration! The Satos are going out to eat tonight. You pick, Tamiko!" Mom said.

"Woot!" I replied. "Burger Johnny's!"

"You sure you don't want sushi?" Dad asked, because that was his favorite. He thought burgers were junk food, but I knew that Mom would be happy with my choice. Plus, since I was a vegetarian, I didn't eat most kinds of sushi. Burger Johnny's had great veggie burgers.

"Burger Johnny's!" I repeated.

Mom started sorting through the pile of mail. "Look," she said, handing me an envelope. "There's a letter for you from *Bayville Monthly*."

I tore open the envelope and started reading the letter aloud.

> "Dear Tamiko Sato,
> Thank you for entering the Bayville County Youth Arts Contest. We are delighted to inform you that, out of the fifty-nine submissions we received this year, your artwork has been chosen for the grand prize."

A grin spread across my face. Good news never gets old!

"Fifty-nine submissions?" my dad repeated. "That means they chose your artwork over fifty-eight others. That's very impressive, Tamiko."

"I didn't even think of that," I said, my grin getting wider. Then I continued reading the letter:

"The county of Bayville would like
to commemorate your artwork by
presenting you with a certificate of
achievement at the town council meeting
next Tuesday. We hope you will be able to
attend.
Congratulations again on your
achievement, and thank you for
supporting *Bayville Monthly*.

Sincerely,
Samantha Dubbins
Editor in Chief, *Bayville Monthly*"

"A certificate of achievement . . . Isn't that kind of
like an award? In front of the whole town?" I asked.

Mom nodded. "Well, in front of whoever shows
up for the meeting. I wonder if Grandma Sasaki will
be able to join us. She would be so proud!"

"I'm going to record the ceremony on my phone
and send it to Grandpa Sato," my father said.

"Yes!" I beamed and made a mental note to invite
Allie and Sierra to the town council meeting too.

We picked Kai up from his business club meeting
before heading to Burger Johnny's.

When I told my brother the good news, his eyes lit

up. "Nice going, Sis!" he said, giving me a fist bump. I almost thought that he was back to being himself, but then he got quiet again. By the time we got to the restaurant and our food had arrived, Kai wasn't even pretending to listen to our conversation anymore.

We were seated around a table in the very noisy burger restaurant, with oldies music blaring from the speakers. I was not into oldies, but Burger Johnny's had the biggest, juiciest veggie burgers and the yummiest french fries.

For the first part of the meal, the main topic of conversation was me, of course.

"This is a very nice affirmation of your talents, Tamiko," Mom went on. "Maybe we need to get you some art lessons, so you can really develop them."

I shook my head. "I don't need lessons. I have natural talent. I had a whole year of art last year, and I didn't learn anything from boring Mr. Rivera."

"Well, maybe he didn't help with your creativity, but I think your techniques have improved," Mom said. "Just think about it, Tamiko. Even creative people need training."

I ignored her and bit into my burger. "Mmm. Maybe my cover entry for next year will be about this place. Do you think they let you win twice? I mean, why not?"

There was a pause in the conversation, so I nudged Kai. "How's your blue cheese burger? I've always wanted to try that one, but I'm on the fence about blue cheese. On the one hand, it tastes good. On the other hand, it looks like something you blow out of your nose."

Kai shrugged and didn't say anything.

I put down my burger. "All right," I said. "Who are you, and what have you done with my brother, Kai? Because this person sitting here is not acting like Kai."

"Very funny, Tamiko," Kai said, rolling his eyes.

"Come on," I pressed. "Why don't you tell me what's going on with you?"

Mom and Dad had their eyes on Kai, and I guessed they'd tried to ask him what was wrong before, without getting any answers.

"Nothing is wrong," he said. "Can't I just eat my burger in peace?"

"Fine," I said, but I wasn't planning on giving up. I knew if anyone could get the truth out of Kai, it would be me!

I figured that he might not want my parents to know what was up, so I waited until we got home. Kai headed right for his bedroom, and I knocked on his door.

"Can I come in?" I asked.

"Can I stop you?" he replied.

I entered. Kai was lying on his bed, staring at the ceiling. I sat down on his desk chair.

"Listen, Kai, I know something's bugging you," I said. "Whatever it is, you can tell me."

"I don't know about that," Kai said.

"Well, if you don't talk to me, you're going to need to talk to *somebody*," I told him. "When you become a millionaire businessman—"

"Billionaire," he corrected me.

"*Billionaire* businessman, then you're going to be under a lot of pressure," I said. "Getting help is a sign of strength, not of weakness. You might as well start practicing how to get rid of stress now!"

There was a long pause. Kai continued staring up at the ceiling.

"What's going on?" I asked again.

"Promise not to tell Mom and Dad?" Kai said.

I nodded.

He sighed. "I have a huge crush on this girl in my class."

"That's why you've been acting so weird?" I asked, trying not to sound disappointed. "I thought something was really wrong!"

Kai sat up. "Something *is* really wrong," he said, and then he sighed. "I can't stop thinking about her, and it's super-distracting! Every time I'm around her, I can't speak. I can barely even talk about stuff like homework with her. That's not like me at all! I can usually talk to anybody."

"What's her name?" I asked.

"Layla," Kai murmured, and his face turned redder than the strawberry ice cream we serve at Molly's.

Now, I was not a big fan of romance, and normally I would have walked backward out of Kai's room and told him to talk to someone else. But I was on such a roll lately, slaying everything I tried. So I decided to give being a romance coach a go.

"You've got the perfect excuse for asking Layla out on a date," I said. "Your sister works at Molly's Ice Cream shop. Use that as an icebreaker and then invite her to get ice cream with you. Nobody says no to ice cream!"

Kai frowned. "Do you think that would work?"

"Why not?" I asked. "It's super-casual, not like going to a movie or to dinner. You could start out by asking if she has any brothers or sisters, and then talk about me and how I work at Molly's."

Kai nodded. "It makes sense. But what if I clam up? Every time I'm around her I get tongue-tied."

"You must have learned strategies in your business club for giving speeches and negotiating and stuff," I said.

"Yeah, you're right!" Kai said. "I could apply some of those things to talking to Layla. Why didn't I think of that?"

"Because you're not a naturally talented problem solver, like I am," I said.

Kai raised his eyebrows, but he didn't argue. "Thanks, Tamiko! Maybe I'll give it a try."

I went back to my room, feeling pretty proud of myself. I'd gotten Kai to open up to me, and I'd even given him some advice that he liked!

Feeling confident, I opened up my planner and checked to see what homework I needed to do. There was a social studies worksheet, a chapter to read for English, and a reminder to study for my Spanish test.

*I don't need to bother studying*, I thought, *and the other stuff won't take long*. So I picked up my phone and tried to find out more about Kai's crush, Layla. I didn't know her last name, but I took a gamble that she might be the only Layla in Kai's grade and searched for Laylas from their high school. It didn't take long before I found her on SuperSnap: Layla Mercedes.

"Okay, Kai, she's cute," I mused out loud. She had curly dark hair and smooth skin without a pimple in sight. Unfortunately, that was all I knew about her, because her profile was set to private, and she didn't have any public posts. None! "All right, mysterious Layla, you can keep your secrets for now," I said. "But Kai had better bring you to Molly's soon!"

## CHAPTER SIX
# I'M A CELEBRITY!

"Tamiko, package for you!"

I ran down the stairs on Saturday afternoon, my head still wet from my shower. I'd finished ninth again in my cross-country meet that morning, and I was getting ready for a chill afternoon of customizing before my shift at Molly's the next day. At first I couldn't imagine what the package could be.

Mom had brought in the mail and handed me a small box. "You ordered something?" she asked.

Then I remembered.

"I still had money left on the gift card Grandma got me for my birthday," I told her, and I ripped open the package. Then I pulled out a pair of black sunglasses and tried them on.

"What do you think?" I asked, putting my hands on my hips and posing.

Mom raised her eyebrows. "They're . . . big, Tamiko. What happened to your other sunglasses?"

"This is a knockoff of a brand that all the celebrities are wearing," I told her. "After the town council meeting my picture will be in the newspaper, and you know, things might get intense."

Mom made a face like she was trying not to smile. "I think you may be overestimating things a bit, sweetie. People get their picture in the paper all the time, and they don't get swarmed by paparazzi afterward."

"You never know," I replied. "I'm like a celebrity at school now. Principal Harrison made an announcement about me over the speakers on Wednesday, and I had, like, a million people come up to me after class. It was amazing."

"A million?" Mom repeated.

"You know what I mean," I said. "Anyway, these sunglasses protect you from UVA *and* UVB rays, and as captain of the Sunscreen Police, you should appreciate that."

Mom sighed. "It's your birthday money, Tamiko.

But you might want to go look in the mirror."

I held out my phone and switched to selfie mode. Mom was right—the glasses were big, and they made my head look small in comparison. But they also looked very glamorous, I thought. I struck a movie-star pose and snapped a picture.

"This is going on the blog!" I announced.

"Of course it is," Mom said in a deadpan voice.

I could tell that Mom didn't like them, but I didn't care. I felt really confident in them. After I dried my hair, I retook the selfie and posted it on my blog. I started getting likes right away, and I knew the sunglasses were a hit. Maybe I could start wearing the sunglasses in all my blog photos instead of covering my face with bunny emojis.

The next day I wore my new sunglasses to my shift at Molly's. When Dad dropped me off, I saw Mrs. S. standing in the window of the shop, taping a large poster to the inside of the window. I grinned. She'd blown up the cover of *Bayville Monthly* with my artwork on it! And next to it she'd printed out my photo with the words: "Congratulations to Our Talented Employee, Tamiko!"

When she saw me, she put down the tape she was holding and rushed over to hug me.

"Tamiko, I can't thank you enough!" she said. "I've tried to get Molly's on the cover before, but I never had any luck. Not only is your artwork really awesome, but it's also been very good for business so far."

"Mom said that yesterday about twenty people said they came because of the new *Bayville Monthly* issue," Allie chimed in.

"I bet we'll *double* that today," I said, as Sierra rushed in.

"Two minutes to spare!" she said proudly. Then she did a double take at me. "Why are you wearing sunglasses inside?"

"Oh, these?" I said, taking them off. "Sorry. They feel so natural that I forgot I had them on."

"You look like a movie star in them," Allie remarked.

"Movie star, social media star, art star, ice cream star—it's kind of all the same, isn't it?" I asked.

Allie raised her eyebrows just as a woman walked through the door. I scooted behind the counter and put on my apron.

"Welcome to world-famous Molly's Ice Cream," I

said. "Can I interest you in our fall special, the pumpkin ginger sundae?"

"That sounds delicious," she replied.

I grinned at Allie. "One pumpkin ginger sundae!"

Allie handed me a cup with two scoops of Pumpkin Caramel Swirl ice cream, I added the toppings, and then things got kind of crazy as more customers streamed through the door. The shop got busy much more quickly than on a normal Sunday. I even saw people walking past stop to read the poster and then come inside.

As I churned out pumpkin ginger sundaes, I kept an eye out for Kai and Layla. The day before, I'd tried asking Kai if he was planning on bringing Layla to Molly's, but he was back to being the quiet, surly Kai who didn't answer my questions.

About an hour in, I saw Kai walk through the door, and my heart skipped a beat. Would I finally get to meet Layla? Were they on a date? Would my brother become happy Kai again?

But I didn't see a pretty dark-haired girl with him, just his friend Matt.

"Where's Layla?" I asked.

"It didn't work out for today," he mumbled,

avoiding my gaze. "Can I have a vanilla cone, please?"

*Uh-oh,* I thought. This was definitely not happy Kai. I gave the order to Allie. Then I nodded to Kai's friend. "What do you want, Matt?"

"What's good?" Matt asked.

"Allie, one pumpkin ginger sundae!" I called out.

Matt pointed toward the window. "Did you really make that cover, Tamiko? That's awesome!"

"Yes, that's me," I said.

The woman waiting behind Matt looked at me. "You're the girl in the window. That's such a lovely collage. Good job!"

A guy behind her chimed in, "Yeah. I got hungry just looking at that cover. This is my third day here in a row!"

"Then maybe you need three scoops today," I said.

As the day went on, lots more people recognized me from the photo and complimented me on the magazine cover.

"You're very talented for such a young lady," a white-haired woman told me.

"You're the girl in the photo! You should be very proud of that cover," said a mom with two toddlers hanging from her elbows.

And more than one person told me that they'd come to the shop for the first time because of the cover!

"Wow," Allie remarked when the rush had died down. "You're super-popular today, Tamiko. You're like a celebrity!"

A rush of confidence and silliness swept over me. I walked over to a drawer and pulled out a paper crown a little boy had left behind after celebrating his birthday at Molly's. (We thought maybe his mom would return for it, but she never did.) I put the crown on my head and lifted my chin high in the air.

"This will have to do until one of my royal subjects makes me a proper crown," I said. "You've met the queen of social media. Now meet the queen of Bayville!" Then I said, in a haughty voice, "Hello, my royal subjects. Bow down to your queen!"

I expected Allie and Sierra to laugh, but they just looked at each other.

"*Chica,* I don't bow to anyone," Sierra said.

"Wow, if I *were* your queen, I'd command you to have a sense of humor," I said. "Lighten up, royal subjects."

They didn't say anything, and I started wiping off the counters.

"If things got this crazy today, I can just imagine what they'll be like at the town council meeting on Tuesday," I mused out loud. "It's a good thing I got these sunglasses. I'm sure I'll be recognized all over town!"

I turned to Sierra and Allie. "You guys are coming, right? My grandma is going to be there, and she hasn't seen either of you in ages."

"We're working late on Tuesday to get the newspaper out," Allie replied. "Sorry."

"And I don't think I'll get out of soccer practice on time," Sierra answered.

"Sure, whatever," I said, and I returned to cleaning the counter. I scrubbed harder and harder as I thought about their answers.

*Allie can't leave her newspaper thing early to come see me? And Sierra doesn't think she'll get out of practice on time? Doesn't it always end at the same time?* It was like they were both giving me excuses not to be there.

*Aren't my friends even happy for me?* I wondered.

## CHAPTER SEVEN

# MIKO AND KIKO

When I got home from my shift, I found Mom reading a book in the living room.

"Mom, I was thinking," I began. "I should get a new dress for the town council meeting."

"I don't think that's necessary," Mom said. "You have plenty of nice clothes, Tamiko."

"But I can't just wear *anything*," I protested. "It's a special event!"

"Tamiko, there's got to be something in your closet already," Mom said.

"I have school clothes, and fancy party clothes, but I don't have getting-honored-at-a-town-council-meeting clothes," I replied.

"You just need to wear a nice dress," Mom said.

"Or a skirt and blouse. Or maybe a blazer. Or—"

Her cell phone rang, and she looked at it. "It's Aunt Kiko. Hold on," Mom said.

Aunt Kiko was my mom's younger sister, and she was *way* cooler than Mom. She had a bright pink streak in her hair and a tiny diamond stud in her nose.

"Yes, Mom is coming tomorrow," my mom was saying. "She'll be staying a couple of nights. . . . Yes, it is a big deal. . . . Sure. She's right here. I was just arguing with her about what she should wear. Hold on."

Mom handed me the phone. "Hey, Miko! Great job winning the art contest," Aunt Kiko said. She liked to call me "Miko" because our names rhymed. When I was a little girl, she would pick me up and spin me around, and we'd say, "Kiko and Miko! Kiko and Miko!" over and over again.

"Thanks," I said. "I was just telling Mom that I need a special dress for Tuesday night, because it's a big deal."

"You definitely need a special dress," Aunt Kiko agreed. "Hey, I'm sorry I can't be there Tuesday night, but there's no way I can get there in time from DC after work."

"I understand," I said.

63

"That's why I drove down today," she said.

I frowned. "What do you mean?"

"Look outside," she said.

Puzzled, I went to the front window and gazed out. There was her red car parked in the driveway.

I squealed. "Mom! She's here!"

"What?" Mom asked.

I ran outside and tackled Aunt Kiko in a hug. "I can't believe you're here!"

"I had a free afternoon, so I thought, *Why not go congratulate Miko in person?*" she said. "I've got to drive back tonight, though."

Mom had followed me outside. "You could have called," she said.

"Nice to see you too, Sis," Aunt Kiko said with a grin. "I didn't think you'd mind. I haven't seen you guys in a while. I missed your squishy face."

Mom shook her head at this, but she was grinning. Mom liked to act like Aunt Kiko annoyed her, but I knew that Mom loved her a lot. "Come on in."

Aunt Kiko raised an eyebrow in a devilish way. "Why don't I kidnap Miko first and take her dress shopping?" she asked.

I jumped up and down. "Yes, yes, yes!"

Mom sighed. "Fine! But, Tamiko, when you grow up to be a spoiled adult, don't blame me," she said. "Have you finished all your homework this weekend?"

I ran through my homework in my mind. Señora Hernandez had given us a worksheet for the Spanish test, but I wasn't worried about studying for that test. I'd already aced the quiz.

"All done," I said, which was true as far as I was concerned.

"Have fun, then," Mom said. "Dinner's at seven."

I happily climbed into Aunt Kiko's car with her, and she drove right to the mall.

"I've been loving your blog, Miko," she told me. "Sounds like things are going well for you. Which, considering you're in middle school, is kind of impressive."

I shrugged. "Is there some rule that you have to have a terrible time in middle school?" I asked.

"Not a rule, but your mom and I both had a terrible time," she said.

"Even you?" I asked. "But you're so cool!"

Aunt Kiko laughed. "I wasn't then. And anyway, when you're one of the only Asian kids in your class, honestly, people don't always think you're cool."

I let that sink in. I knew that Aunt Kiko and Mom had grown up as the only Japanese Americans in their school, but I had never really thought about it until now.

"Are there a lot of other Asian kids at your school?" Aunt Kiko asked.

"There are some Asian Americans, but I'm the only Japanese American," I answered.

I thought about it a little more. Sometimes my classmates would make stereotypical comments like, "But I thought all Asian kids were good at math." And back in fifth grade whenever Mom packed me Japanese food, Bryan Fox would point at it and yell, "Ew! Gross!" But thankfully, I'd never been really bullied for being Japanese. There were all kinds of kids at MLK, so people were mostly respectful.

"At MLK I don't actually stick out unless I wear a really crazy outfit," I added.

"That's a good thing," Aunt Kiko said. "It's why your mom and dad wanted you and Kai to go to MLK."

"Wait, what?" I asked. "It's not like we have a choice. It's because of where we live."

"Right," Aunt Kiko said. "When Kai was a baby, your parents looked for a house close to where your mom and I grew up, and where Grandma Sasaki lives now. But they also didn't want Kai to feel left out at school. That's why they ended up moving to Bayville and picking the house you're in now, so Kai and you could go to MLK."

"They never told us that," I said, and my mind started going in a million directions. It hadn't occurred to me that my parents had purposely wanted me to go to MLK. I had never felt particularly proud of the school, especially not after Allie had transferred to Vista Green. I was even a little jealous that her school had a state-of-the-art media room and delicious lunches. But the more I thought about it, the more I couldn't imagine being a student anywhere besides at MLK. And anyway, if I hadn't lived in Bayville, I never would have met Sierra or Allie. And that would have been *tragic*!

Aunt Kiko looked at me. "Whoa, didn't mean to blow your mind."

I shook my head. "No, it's okay. I'm glad I go to MLK," I replied. *Who needs avocado toast and a brand-new laptop every year?*

She laughed as we pulled into the mall parking lot. "Any good stores in here?" she asked.

"A few," I said. I paused. "This is really nice of you. Thanks!"

She grinned. "I don't get to spend enough time with you. Your contest win was the little push I needed to come down and visit you."

We entered the mall and headed to Stardust, a new shop that sold everything from semiformal dresses to fancy prom and bridesmaids' stuff.

"Wow, this is all so . . . sparkly," Aunt Kiko said. "This is a town council meeting, right?"

"Not all of the dresses are sparkly," I promised, and I led her to the area of semiformal dresses.

First I tried on a very classy black dress with cap sleeves and a wide skirt.

"Very glamorous," Aunt Kiko said. "But the cover you designed is so cute and colorful! Maybe your dress should match."

"I like that idea," I agreed, and after trying on a few more dresses, we agreed on a petal-pink dress with lace on top and a skirt that fell to just below my knees.

"You look beautiful, Miko," Aunt Kiko said. "Like

a strawberry ice cream cone. It's not overly fancy, either. Do you have shoes that go with it?"

I visualized my closet and remembered I had a pair of pink flats. "I'm good!"

Aunt Kiko paid for the dress, and we walked around the mall for a while, talking and window-shopping. Aunt Kiko told me about the new exhibit at the art gallery in Washington, DC, where she works, and I told her about working in the ice cream shop.

"How's Kai doing?" she asked, and I found myself spilling the tea about the whole Layla situation.

"I *told* him that bringing her to Molly's would be the perfect date, and he showed up with Matt," I said, shaking my head. "Why didn't he listen to me?"

"Older siblings never take advice from younger siblings," Aunt Kiko replied. "Believe me, your mom never listens to me."

I laughed. "You mean it never changes?"

"I haven't given up hope," Aunt Kiko said. "But then again, she let me bring you here today. So maybe I'm finally winning."

"I think I'm the one winning today," I said, looking down at the bag that held my beautiful new dress.

She looked at her watch. "We should get back to the house. What's your mom cooking?"

I shook my head. "No idea. But it's Sunday, so it'll probably be something Japanese."

My dad was born in Tokyo and came to America to go to college, where he met my mom. My mom was born here, so she liked to mostly eat and cook American food. But my dad missed the food from Tokyo, so Mom made it for us a few times a week, and just about every Sunday.

We returned home to the scent of something delicious coming from the kitchen and found Mom cooking pancakes on the stove.

"Okonomiyaki!" Aunt Kiko squealed.

"I know they're your favorite, and I wanted to thank you for getting Tamiko a dress," she said. "They're almost done."

Okonomiyaki was a kind of Japanese pancake filled with vegetables and meat, and topped with dried fish flakes and seaweed, plus a special sauce and mayonnaise. (My mom made a special vegetarian version for me.) It was really delicious. Dad had told me that "*okonomiyaki*" meant "what you like," so you could put whatever you wanted into the pancake. Mom did it Dad's favorite way, which meant she used lots of crispy cabbage, red peppers, green onions, and chopped-up shrimp. It was the ultimate comfort food!

"Tamiko, before you help your brother set the table, show me the dress!" Mom said.

I took it out of the bag and held it up in front of me. "What do you think?"

"Very pretty," Mom said. "Thanks again, Kiko!"

Aunt Kiko ate dinner with us, and we all stayed up pretty late for a Sunday, because everyone was having so much fun talking that she didn't want to leave. I woke up extra yawny on Monday and tuned out during most of my classes. And on Monday afternoon the family fun continued because Grandma Sasaki, my mom's mom, arrived right after Kai and I got back from school.

"Tamiko! Kai! Where are my beautiful grandchildren?" she cried as she came through the front door, carrying a duffel bag and a shopping bag.

I ran downstairs to hug her. Her head of curly gray hair was just about even with mine.

"Grandma, you're here!" I said, stepping back from her. "Nice jogging suit."

I was half teasing, because Grandma always wore jogging suits, and today her suit was as yellow as a lemon.

"It's my Tamiko, the big winner!" she cried, giving me another hug. "I'm so proud of you."

"Thanks, Grandma," I said.

"Take this up to the guest room, please," she said, handing me the duffel bag. Then she held up the shopping bag. "Then come on down and help me with dinner. I brought my pickles!"

"Okay!" I said, and I ran up the stairs, happy and excited. First Aunt Kiko had come for a visit, and now Grandma had driven almost three hours just to see me get my award. I felt like a superstar!

Grandma made us Japanese omelets and rice and her pickled vegetables for dinner, and we talked about the ceremony happening the next night.

"We should get there early," I said. "Just to make sure we can all get seats."

"I'm sure there will be plenty of seats," Mom said.

"I don't know," I said. "There might be a lot of people there."

"I don't think there's anything big on the agenda tomorrow," Dad said.

72

I raised my eyebrows. "Yes, there is. Me!"

"That's my confident girl," Grandma Sasaki said, and I beamed at her. "I am lucky to have two such talented grandchildren. Kai, what is the business club doing this year?"

Kai didn't look up from his plate. "Um, nothing planned yet, Grandma," he said.

Grandma looked at Mom. "What is the matter with him? Is he sick?"

"No, he's—" I started to answer but stopped myself. Kai would have been furious if I'd told everyone about his feelings for Layla.

"He's a teen, Mom. You know how that goes," my mom replied, and Grandma Sasaki nodded.

"Yes, moody," she said. "He probably gets it from you."

Mom sighed. "Here we go. . . ."

Grandma Sasaki spent the next hour telling us stories about Mom and Aunt Kiko when they were teenagers. By the time we finished dinner and I helped clean up, it was getting late. I excused myself to do homework. First I did a math sheet and read a chapter of a novel for English. I checked my planner.

"Spanish test tomorrow!" it said.

"I'll ace it," I told myself, and I climbed into bed. Soon I drifted off to sleep. In my dreams I was walking down the stairs of town hall in my pink dress, as adoring fans cheered loudly and tossed roses at my feet. . . .

## CHAPTER EIGHT
# THE BIG NIGHT!

"Conjugate the word in the future tense." I squinted at my Spanish test and frowned. Hmm. I couldn't remember learning the words on the list in the future tense. Had I missed something? I thought I'd been paying attention in class.

*I think you just add an* e *with an accent mark at the end of the word,* I thought, and I quickly breezed through the word list.

There was an essay question too. This time we had to write about three jobs that we might want in the future. I didn't know how to say "social media manager" or "fashion designer," so I used a lot of English words. I thought it looked pretty good; I'd used some English words on the quiz, and I'd gotten a perfect score!

Señora Hernandez raised an eyebrow when I handed my paper in before everyone else, but she didn't question me. I went back to my desk and started to doodle in my notebook.

Tamiko Sato

Tamiko Sato

Tamiko Sato

I wrote my signature over and over, practicing in case anybody asked me to autograph their issue of *Bayville Monthly* magazine. I tried starting with a little curl at the start of my *T*, or a flourish at the end of both *O*s, or turning both *O*s into hearts.

At lunchtime I showed my favorite three signatures to Sierra and MacKenzie.

"What do you think?" I asked. "I'm trying to perfect my signature."

"The hearts are cute," Sierra said, "but they kind of look like *U*s too. So people might think your name is Tamiku Satu."

I frowned. "That sounds terrible!"

MacKenzie pointed to one of my attempts. "I like the way that one looks," she said. "Is that, like, an artist's signature or something?"

"It could be," I said. "But mainly I'm practicing in case I need to sign autographs tonight."

"What's tonight?" MacKenzie asked.

"Don't you know? I'm being recognized at the town council meeting for my *Bayville Monthly* cover. Sierra can't go," I said with a glance at Sierra, "but you should come! I'll save you a seat."

"I don't know," MacKenzie said. "I've got to work on my social studies project tonight."

"You can work on that later," I said, and then I raised my voice, so other kids in the cafeteria could hear me. "Anybody can come to the town council meeting tonight to see me get recognized for winning the *Bayville Monthly* cover contest. It would be nice to see some MLK kids there to cheer me on."

A few kids turned their heads to look at me, and I knew I'd gotten my point across. But I swear I saw Sierra roll her eyes!

"Don't worry about missing it, Si," I said. "I'm

going to get Kai to take lots of pictures, and I'll send them to you."

"I'm sure you will," Sierra replied, and MacKenzie started talking about her social studies project again.

It was hard to focus during the rest of the day, and when school ended, Grandma Sasaki picked me up so I wouldn't have to take the bus. The council meeting wasn't until seven, but I started to get ready. I showered and washed my hair. Then I curled the ends so they looked nice and bouncy. I put on sweats and a T-shirt as we ate an early dinner, and then at six o'clock I put on the new pink dress.

I took a mirror selfie and posted it to my blog.

On my way to a ceremony honoring me for winning an art contest! Wearing an #IceCream colored dress to show the love for #MollysIceCream. Life is sweet!

"Tamiko, time to go!" Mom called upstairs.

I came down and saw that everyone was dressed up. Dad and Kai were wearing button-down shirts. Mom was wearing a really nice black dress, and Grandma was wearing a flowered blouse and tan pants—no jogging suit! And she was doing it just for me! I felt really special.

We piled into Dad's car and headed to the town hall.

Bayville Town Hall was a beautiful old brick building with tall white columns in front. It was located in the beach district, near the shops and Molly's Ice Cream. It was a warm night, and the streets were still crowded with people shopping and going to restaurants.

We parked and walked up to the building. Mom and Dad saw someone they knew and started talking while Kai, Grandma, and I waited to go inside with them. I scanned the people waiting for the meeting, looking for any of my classmates or friends. I didn't recognize anyone—in fact, Kai and I were the only kids—but maybe my fans were just running late.

Then, across the street, I saw Ewan!

"Ewan!" I called out. Ewan looked surprised to see me. He glanced both ways before crossing the street.

"Hey, Tamiko," he said. "You look nice."

"Thanks," I said. "It's so nice of you to come cheer me on. I had no idea you would show up."

Ewan looked confused. "I was just on my way back from the library," he said. "I didn't know anything was happening at the town hall with you. . . . Is that why you're dressed up?"

*Ewan isn't here for me?* My cheeks started to burn.

79

"Yeah," I said. "I'm being recognized at the town council meeting for winning the *Bayville Monthly* contest."

"Oh right," Ewan said. There was a pause as he fidgeted with the collar on his shirt. "I wish I could, um, stay, but my mom is expecting me home. Congratulations, though!"

"Thanks!" I said cheerfully, but I cringed inside as he walked away. I had assumed that Ewan would stay and support me. How embarrassing!

Kai tapped my arm. "Tamiko, we're going in."

I followed my family into the building, and a woman in a blue suit walked up to me.

"You must be Tamiko!" she said. "My, you look lovely. I'm Samantha Dubbins from *Bayville Monthly*. We really love your cover, Tamiko."

"Thank you," I replied. "Nice to meet you, Ms. Dubbins."

She looked at my entourage. "You must be Tamiko's family. We've saved some seats up front for everyone. The recognition ceremony is early in the meeting agenda, and then you can leave if you want."

"What's going to happen?" I asked. "Do we need to rehearse?"

Ms. Dubbins laughed. "It's not that complicated. Just come to the front of the room with me when Mayor Ford calls us up."

I nodded, and I glanced around as we took our seats. Most of the people there were wearing casual clothes. There were even a few guys in shorts! I felt a little overdressed, but I didn't let that bother me. I knew I looked great!

At the very front of the room and seated behind a long table were, I guess, the town council members. They looked a little better-dressed than the people in the audience. Two of the men wore suit jackets, and the women wore very nice blouses. The man sitting behind the little sign that read MAYOR FORD had a neatly trimmed gray beard and wore a blue suit jacket over a blue-and-red plaid shirt.

At seven o'clock a little bell chimed. Mayor Ford stood up and said, "Please rise for the Pledge of Allegiance."

I glanced around some more during the Pledge of Allegiance. Nearly every seat in the hall was filled! I imagined what I'd say to my fans when they approached me.

"It's a real honor. I'm proud to be from Bayville!"

"Thanks. It was a combination of natural talent and hard work."

"Yes, I'd love to be in your TV commercial. . . ."

Mayor Ford made some boring announcements that I barely paid attention to. Then he said, "And now for our public comment portion."

A lot of the people in the room stood and lined up behind a microphone on the side of the room. One by one they walked up and started complaining.

"We really need a traffic light on Maple Avenue. The stop sign isn't enough!"

"My neighbor leaves out his garbage two days before pickup. I've called the police, but they won't do anything."

"The dogs at the dog park make too much noise!"

I tapped my foot impatiently. When would they stop? And it bothered me that once they stopped complaining, they left the room. My audience was dwindling!

Finally the last complainer finished. Mayor Ford looked at the agenda.

"Let's start with our first agenda item tonight. We're going to formally congratulate Ms. Tamiko Sato, an eighth grader at MLK Middle School. Her collage, inspired by Molly's Ice Cream parlor here in Bayville, won *Bayville Monthly*'s annual cover contest. I must say, I really enjoy Molly's Maple Butter Pecan flavor!"

Everybody laughed.

"I'd like to call up Tamiko and Ms. Dubbins from *Bayville Monthly*," he said.

I walked up onto the stage with Ms. Dubbins, and she led me over to Mayor Ford. Everyone in the hall started clapping.

"Tamiko, the town of Bayville would like to present you with this certificate of recognition for contributing to Bayville tourism," he said, handing me a fancy piece of paper.

"And *Bayville Monthly* would like to present you with this framed edition of the magazine," Samantha added. She handed that to me too.

Then a photographer walked up to us, carrying a professional camera with big flashes.

"Okay, everybody, big smiles! Little girl, hold up the certificate, please," he said.

*Little girl!* I was insulted, but I obeyed and gave my best smile. Mom, Dad, and Kai stood up and started taking pictures with their phones. Everyone clapped some more.

Then Ms. Dubbins motioned that it was time to step down, and I followed her off the stage. I went back to my row in the audience but didn't sit down.

"Let's go," I hissed, but Mom shook her head and motioned for me to sit.

"Why?" I asked.

Grandma Sasaki leaned across Mom. "Because it is rude to leave. We must stay for the meeting."

"But those other people left!" I protested.

"If those other people jumped off a bridge, would you do that, too?" Grandma Sasaki asked, and I knew there was no arguing. I sat down in my seat and slumped.

The big moment was over. Instead of being surrounded by adoring fans, I was sitting in an uncomfortable chair and listening to some bald guy talk about the town sewer system.

I sighed. This ceremony had not gone as I'd expected. I mean, the recognition was nice. But although the hall had been filled with people, none of my friends or classmates had come to see me! And how embarrassing was it when I thought Ewan was here for me but I was wrong? I couldn't believe he didn't even know I was getting an award!

I thought back to the exchange with Ewan. *What did he mean, he didn't know about the ceremony? Doesn't he read my blog? Didn't he hear me in the cafeteria?*

I got madder and madder at Ewan and my friends the longer the meeting went on. My anger was all their fault. What kind of friends were they to not support me in my time of glory?

When the meeting was finally over, I practically ran outside.

"What's the hurry, Tamiko?" Dad said.

"I just want to go home," I snapped.

"Really? I thought we could go to Molly's to celebrate," Dad said.

I shook my head. Not even ice cream could change my sour mood into a sweet one. "I don't feel like it."

Mom and Grandma looked at each other.

"Moody," Mom said, and Grandma nodded.

I didn't argue with them.

# CHAPTER NINE
# LAYLA, AT LAST

On the way home I made sure Mom, Dad, and Kai texted me all the photos they'd taken. I sent some of the best ones to Sierra and Allie that night before I went to sleep.

**You look beautiful, Tamiko!** Allie replied.

**Muy bonita, chica!** 😎 Sierra wrote.

Their replies made me smile, but I was still kind of annoyed with them.

**I missed you tonight, but you can make it up to me. Come over one day after school?** I wrote back.

**I can do tomorrow or Thursday!** Allie responded right away.

**What about you, Sierra? Can you squeeze me into your schedule?**

Chill! Sierra responded. Thursday is free for me.

See you Thursday. I'll see if Mom will order us Thai food, I replied, confident that Mom would say yes. She liked it when Allie, Sierra, and me got together, especially since we didn't see Allie every day anymore.

Then, exhausted, I drifted off to sleep. This time I dreamed that I was trapped inside the town hall, and the line of people complaining about stuff stretched out the door for miles, and miles, and miles. . . .

On Thursday, Sierra took the bus home with me. We got out just as Allie's dad pulled up and Allie got out of the car.

"Sprinkle Sundays sisters on a Thursday!" I cried, and the three of us hugged.

"Pick you up later, Allie!" Mr. Shear said, and he drove off.

"I have to be home by seven," Sierra said. "I have so much homework! I miss the summer already!"

"I've got a ton of homework too," Allie agreed, and then she held up the white paper bag she was holding. "I brought a pint of Apple Pie ice cream."

"Yes!" I cried. "This more than makes up for you guys missing my ceremony the other night."

Allie and Sierra exchanged glances.

"Yeah, well, you know we couldn't help it," Allie said.

Sierra took the bag from Allie. "Come on. Let's crack this open. I'm ravenous!"

We walked into the house, and everyone dumped their backpacks onto the front hallway bench. My dad was still at work, but I heard my mom call hello from upstairs. I'd said good-bye to Grandma Sasaki that morning, so I figured the kitchen would be empty. Kai usually had some kind of meeting after school these days.

But when we walked into the kitchen, there was Kai, seated at the kitchen table with a girl! A girl with dark, curly hair and gorgeous, glowing skin. I recognized her right away from her SuperSnap photo. It was Layla! Both Kai and Layla had their textbooks open, and I figured they were doing homework.

"Hi, Kai," Sierra said.

"Oh, hi," Kai said, and he looked startled. "I didn't know you all were—hi."

I waited for Kai to introduce Layla, but he seemed stalled. So I stepped up.

"I'm Tamiko, Kai's sister," I said. "I'm sure he's told

you all about me. And these are my friends Sierra and Allie."

"I'm Layla," she replied, a little bit shyly. "Nice to meet you."

"Homework session?" I asked, trying not to roll my eyes. Why would Kai invite a girl to do homework? Why wouldn't he bring her to Molly's, like I'd suggested?

"Yes, we're studying for an algebra test," Kai replied. Then he gave me a look that clearly said, *Get out of here!*

"We're going upstairs, but first we're going to have some Apple Pie ice cream that Allie brought from Molly's," I said. For Layla I added, "Allie's mom owns the place, and the three of us work there."

"That's nice," Layla replied.

"Have you had Molly's ice cream before?" I asked. Layla shook her head, and I gasped. "That's ridiculous! You're seriously missing out."

I started taking bowls out of the cabinet. After Allie scooped ice cream into the first bowl, I brought it over to Layla. "Here you go. It's delicious! One of our fabulous fall flavors."

"No, thanks," Layla replied.

*What is wrong with this girl?* I thought. *Who doesn't like ice cream?* But I gave her a big smile. If anyone could convince Layla to try the ice cream, it would be me, the ice cream queen!

"Oh, come on. You'll love it!" I assured her, and I slid the bowl over to her. To my amazement, she pushed it back toward me. "You have to trust me on this. Allie's mom uses all-natural and a lot of local ingredients. She makes fresh ice cream every day. It's like nothing you've ever tasted," I insisted, and pushed the bowl back toward her. I really wanted her to at least *try* it.

Allie gave a bowl to Kai, who was watching me and Layla with a look of distress on his face.

"Thanks, but I honestly don't want any ice cream," Layla said to me.

"Just one taste, and you'll want more," I pressed. She was hurting my pride as Molly's unofficial marketing director!

Layla looked completely uncomfortable now. "Really, I don't—"

Now I was getting really annoyed with her. I glanced over at Kai, who was starting to take a bite of his ice cream. "Oh, I get it," I interrupted Layla.

"You don't want your *own* bowl, because you want an excuse to share with my brother."

"Tamiko!" Sierra hissed behind me. Kai turned bright red, his spoon frozen in the air. Layla almost looked like she might cry—and that's when I knew that I had messed up.

Layla took a deep, shaky breath. "I can't eat any ice cream because I have severe lactose intolerance," she said. Then she lowered her voice. "So please, don't try to force people to eat things. Sometimes they just can't."

Normally I was great at thinking on my feet and coming up with a witty response. Once, I had accidentally spilled a unicorn sundae in front of all the customers at Molly's. But then I'd yelled, "Unicorn down!" which had made everyone laugh and had helped relieve the tension in the air.

But in this moment I had no idea what to say, or how to make the tension better. I wanted to shrink to the size of a mosquito and fly away.

Layla closed her textbook, stuffed it into her bag, and stood up.

"Sorry, Kai. I need to get home before dinner," she mumbled. Then she raced past me out of the kitchen. I could hear the front door open, then slam shut.

## CHAPTER TEN
# THE TRUTH HURTS

"What was that for?" Kai yelled at me. "You ruined everything. Now she's never going to talk to me again!"

I wished I could just disappear. I felt awful.

And I *hate* feeling awful, so I did what I always do: I fought back.

"Don't be so dramatic!" I yelled back. "She could have said something the first time I offered her the ice cream."

Kai slammed his textbook shut. "You're terrible sometimes, Tamiko," he said, and he stormed out of the room.

"You're not so great yourself!" I yelled after him. Then I turned to my friends, embarrassed that he had called me out in front of Allie and Sierra. "Brothers, right? Come on. Let's bring the ice cream up to my room before it melts."

My friends were silent as we walked upstairs.

"Is everything okay?" my mom called from her bedroom. "I heard some yelling."

"Everything's fine," I called back, even though I wasn't 100 percent sure it was true.

Once inside my room, we sat on the rag rug I'd made myself (yes, I can do almost anything!), but before I could get a spoonful of Apple Pie goodness into my mouth, Allie spoke up.

"Tamiko, why did you do that?" she asked.

"What, you mean offer Layla ice cream?" I asked. "I was just trying to help her and Kai break the ice. Kai's been miserable because he really likes her, and he doesn't know how to talk to her. How was I supposed to know she was lactose intolerant?"

"She tried to tell you," Sierra piped up. "But you were being, well, kind of—"

"Pushy," Allie finished for her. "And then you accused her of wanting to share Kai's bowl. . . ."

I flinched a little, remembering that. But I wasn't ready to admit that I'd been wrong. "Come on. That was a joke! Doesn't anybody have a sense of humor anymore?"

"It didn't sound like you were joking," Sierra said.

"Seriously? You guys know I'm the queen of comedy," I said.

Sierra and Allie exchanged glances. They didn't speak for a moment. I put down my ice cream bowl and folded my arms across my chest. "What?" I asked.

"It's just—you've been calling yourself a queen a lot lately," Sierra began. "You know, queen of social media. Ice cream queen. Stuff like that."

"It's just an expression," I said. "Because I'm confident about the things I'm good at. Isn't everybody always saying that girls are supposed to be strong and confident and proud of who we are?"

"Yes," Sierra replied. "And your confidence is a beautiful thing. But sometimes—"

"Look at it this way," Allie interrupted. "Think about all the queens in fairy tales and stories. The Queen of Hearts in *Alice's Adventures in Wonderland*. The wicked queen in *Snow White and the Seven Dwarfs*. They're usually villains."

"And your point is that I'm a villain?" I snapped.

"No. My point is that being confident is one

thing, but being a queen who doesn't care about other people's feelings and orders everyone around is not cool," Allie replied.

"Who says I don't care about other people's feelings?" I asked, my voice rising. How *dare* Allie accuse me of that!

"Well, you were kind of mad at us for not going to your ceremony," Sierra pointed out. "Which wasn't really fair. You know that we love you, but we were just too busy."

I thought about this. I *had* given them both a hard time, and it wasn't really their fault that they'd already had plans.

"I guess it was just really important to me, and I wanted you there," I said.

"Winning the contest is a big deal," Allie said. "But you've been kind of bragging about it ever since it happened. And acting like you're a celebrity, which is a little, you know, *extra.*"

I would have laughed at that if I hadn't still been feeling embarrassed and angry. She was right. If you looked up the word "extra" in the dictionary, you would find my picture there, me wearing my favorite pair of rhinestone sunglasses and fluorescent pink lip gloss.

I took a deep breath. "Okay, maybe I have been a little more excited about it than I should be," I conceded.

"And what happened just now?" Sierra said. "You might have been trying to help, but I don't think you were really thinking about Kai's or Layla's feelings."

"You tried to force Layla to eat something that was harmful to her," Allie added.

"All right, I get it!" I leaned back against my bed and sighed. There was no question that what I'd done to Layla was wrong. "You win. I'll step down from the throne. But if I can't be a queen of everything, can I at least be a princess?"

"How about a knight?" Allie suggested. "You know, fighting for what's right, and doing good deeds and stuff like that."

"The ice cream knight," I said slowly. "It doesn't have the same kind of ring to it as 'ice cream queen.' Maybe I'll just stick with being Tamiko for now."

Then I paused and stared down at my ice cream. "I'm really sorry if I was mean to either of you. Will you forgive me?"

"Of course!" Sierra said.

"Definitely," Allie added, and she held up her

ice cream bowl. "Cheers to friendship!"

We clinked our ice cream bowls together gently, and then I took another spoonful of the Apple Pie ice cream, which was pretty much soup by now, but still delicious.

"This is a really yummy flavor," I said.

Sierra frowned. "Poor Layla! Imagine not being able to eat ice cream!"

"I know," Allie said. "That's why Mom puts strawberry sorbet on the menu in the summer, for people who can't eat dairy."

I nodded. "The sorbet is tasty, but imagine only being able to eat one flavor! And sorbet isn't as creamy as ice cream."

"I'd be really sad if I couldn't eat ice cream," Sierra said. "Or cheese. Or put milk in my cereal."

"Is that true?" Allie asked. "Isn't there special milk for people who are lactose intolerant?"

I shrugged. "I don't know. Let's find out."

We all took out our phones and searched "lactose intolerance."

"Oh my gosh, millions of people have it!" Sierra cried. "And this says that as you get older, you lose your ability to break down the lactose in dairy products. Does this mean no ice cream in our futures?"

"Well, it doesn't kill you, right? Maybe we could eat it anyway," I said.

Allie frowned. "Ugh, it causes lots of nastiness," she said. "Bloating, upset stomach, and more."

I scrolled, trying to look for good news. "Okay, it says some lactose intolerant people can eat yogurt. And some kinds of cheeses, depending on how lactose intolerant you are."

"And there is medicine you can take to help you digest the lactose," Sierra added. "But then there are also people who can't or won't eat dairy at all, so those kinds of products aren't right for them."

I looked down at my empty ice cream bowl and thought about how Layla had said she was severely lactose intolerant. "I hope I never become lactose intolerant," I said. Then I realized something. "Layla probably wished she could try the ice cream. And I made her feel bad. Oh, I'm awful!"

"You're not awful," Sierra said.

"But maybe you can apologize to her," Allie suggested.

I shook my head. "I'll probably never see her

again. Even if she doesn't blame this on Kai, he'll never bring her to the house again. I really messed up!"

"You can at least apologize to Kai," Sierra said. I nodded. That wasn't going to be fun, but I had to do it. I messed up and had to make it right.

Thankfully, Sierra and Allie had other things to talk about besides *me* and what a horrible person I'd become. We ended up having a fun afternoon, a lot like the ones we'd had when we all went to MLK together.

My dad was working late, so Mom ordered Thai food for dinner. Allie had khao pad, which is Thai fried rice. Sierra had coconut curry, and I had pad thai, which is a rice noodle stir-fry. Mom ordered tom yum soup, a kind of hot and sour soup with shrimp.

We all ate in the kitchen, with Kai conspicuously not there.

"Where's Kai at?" I asked Mom casually.

"He went to Kevin's for dinner," Mom replied. I looked over at Sierra and Allie and frowned. He was so mad at me that he'd left the house on *Thai food* night!

"Do you all want dessert?" Mom asked after we'd

eaten our dinner. "We've got some Molly's ice cream in the freezer."

Allie, Sierra, and I looked at one another a little guiltily. *Should I tell Mom we ate our ice cream before dinner?* Then we burst into giggles.

"What's so funny?" Mom asked.

"Nothing—thank you, Mrs. Sato. We're just—full, I guess," Allie said.

"Yeah, too much Thai food," I added, and we burst into giggles again.

Then Allie's dad came to pick up Allie and Sierra. We had a group hug at the door.

"Sprinkle Sundays sisters!" we cried, and I smiled as they got into the car. I felt so much better after our talk. But I still needed to deal with Kai and Layla.

I went into my room to do homework and kept the door cracked open so I would hear Kai come home. After about an hour I heard his footsteps creaking in the hall. I jumped up, walked over to his room, and knocked on the door.

"Go away, Tamiko!" he called out.

"I just want to apologize!" I said. "I was a jerk!"

"Yes, you were a jerk," he said.

"So can I come in?" I asked.

Kai didn't respond. I gently tried the doorknob, but he'd locked the door.

I took a deep breath, not sure what to do.

Kai had never been this mad at me, not even when I was eight and had drawn a mural of dinosaurs on his bedroom wall in crayon.

Would Kai ever forgive the ice cream queen?

## CHAPTER ELEVEN
# UPS AND DOWNS

On Friday morning I did a quick blog post before I left for school. I uploaded a photo of me and Kai in downtown Tokyo, wearing sunglasses. I was making a goofy face, and Kai was smiling.

Flashback to my brother and me in Tokyo this summer. If you are lucky enough to have a big brother, then you know that they're the best!

I wasn't sure if Kai would see it, but it made me feel a little better to do it. I heard him leaving the house before I even got dressed, and I figured he was still too mad to even look at me. Sigh.

My day at school didn't start out much better. Señora Hernandez handed back our Spanish tests, and mine had a big fat C+ on the top.

What had happened? I thought I had aced the test! I scanned the parts where Señora Hernandez had taken points away. All the English words I had used in the essay section were marked with a red *X*.

Then I looked at the word list section, and my stomach sank. The instructions had been to conjugate each verb in the future tense *for all pronouns*, but I had only conjugated them for the "I" pronoun! I couldn't believe I had made such a careless mistake.

At the end of the test, Señora Hernandez had written, *Puedes hacerlo mejor!* Even though I might have been a C+ student, I knew that meant "You can do better!"

I sighed and thought about my talk with Allie and Sierra. This was so embarrassing, especially after getting a perfect score on the quiz. Not only had my overconfidence led me to hurt people's feelings, but it had also made me careless at school. I vowed not to disappoint Señora Hernandez again!

I glanced over at Ewan. I hadn't really hurt his feelings the other night outside town hall, but afterward I'd gotten angry with him for no reason. He'd been really nice to me, and he'd even complimented me on my dress. What had been wrong with me that night?

When class was over, I approached Ewan.

"Hey, I'm sorry if I was weird the other night, when I was waiting for the ceremony outside town hall," I said. "I mean, of course you wouldn't want to go to something boring like that."

Ewan shrugged. "It's okay. I might have gone if I'd known about it."

I smiled, flattered. "Anyway, like I said, I'm sorry if it was awkward," I told him.

He grinned. "Well, I will only accept your apology if you help me with Spanish, Miss Perfect Score," he joked. "It's not my best subject."

I pulled my test out of my backpack and showed it to him. Ewan's eyes widened in surprise.

"I'm not Miss Perfect Score anymore," I said. "But that's because I didn't study. I know I can do better if I work at it."

"Then we should definitely study together sometime," Ewan said. "How about tomorrow? We could meet at the library."

"I, um, I have cross-country in the morning," I said. "But we could meet at around three?"

"Sure," he said. Then he hastily added, "I mean, you won't be too tired, from your race, I mean?"

"Nope, I'll be fine," I assured him. "See you then!" I thought Ewan was blushing a little, but it could've just been a trick of the eye. And then we had to travel in different directions to get to our next classes.

My day was starting to look up. Still, it was hard to shake the bad feeling I had about Kai being angry with me. I checked my blog between math and science class to see if I had any new comments.

Sierra had been the first person to comment on the post. "Love it!"

Allie had commented too: "I wish my brother was as cool as yours!"

That made me giggle. Allie had a younger brother named Tanner. He was still a little kid, and his shirt always had some kind of food stain on it. Allie was always complaining about how he didn't have any manners.

I glanced at a few more comments, but none of them were from Kai. There was no way of knowing if he had seen the post.

I walked into science class feeling a bit gloomy. Mr. O. was wearing a T-shirt that read, WHEN PRO-TONS BATTLE. The image on the shirt showed little black dots carrying swords and yelling, CHARGE!

"So, what do you think of this shirt?" he asked at the start of class. "I was telling my friend about Tamiko's joke about negative energy the other day, and she got this for me."

"I don't get it!" Sierra called out.

"It's the proton battle cry, because they're positively charged," he said.

"Good one, Mr. O.," I said.

"I've got more," he said. "There are tons of jokes about atoms. Did you know that? Like, Why did the proton and the electron go out on a date?"

"Why?" somebody yelled.

"Because opposites attract!" Mr. O. said, and he started cracking up. A lot of kids groaned, but I smiled.

"All right. How about this one?" he asked. "What did the neutron say to the proton in the nucleus?"

"WHAT?" we all shouted.

"I can't believe *Atom* is letting me live here *free of charge*," he said. "Get it? Because neutrons have no charge." Even I groaned at that one, but Mr. O.'s corny jokes put me in a better mood.

When I got home after school and entered the house, I found Kai at the kitchen table doing his homework.

Before he could run away from me, I sat down at the table directly across from him.

"Hi, big brother," I said. "Have I told you today how awesome you are?"

Kai ignored me and kept typing on his laptop.

I went to the cabinet and took out a glass. "You must be thirsty. Here, let me get you a nice glass of cold iced tea."

I poured some for him and placed it next to him. He didn't look up. I sat down across from him and looked at him expectantly. I was going to do whatever it took for him to talk to me again!

Finally he spoke. "Are you just going to stare at me all day? Don't you have anything better to do?"

"Kai, I really am sorry," I said. "So sorry. Let me make it up to you somehow."

Kai sighed. "It's all right, I guess. Layla talked to me today about it. She said she always feels awkward talking about her lactose intolerance. She wanted to tell me when I invited her to Molly's, but she was too embarrassed. So in a way, she's glad it's out in the open."

"Does that mean she's not mad at you or me?" I asked.

Kai thought about it for a second. "No, she didn't

seem mad at me. But if I were her, I'd never want to talk to you again."

I cringed as I remembered Layla, sitting at our kitchen table and looking like she was about to cry. "I feel so bad," I said. "It must really stink not to be able to eat delicious things like ice cream and pizza."

"Yeah. She said that there are some good dairy-free products out there, but they're hard to find," Kai responded. "And forget about finding them at restaurants."

"Well, Molly's does have a strawberry sorbet that's dairy-free," I said. "But that's not exactly exciting if you only have one flavor to choose from."

Kai got that look on his face that he got when he had an idea.

"You know, Molly's should start selling dairy-free ice cream," he said. "There are lots of people with the same condition as Layla. It could bring in new business for the store."

"That is a brilliant idea!" I said, and I texted Allie and Sierra right away.

Kai is speaking to me again! I began. He said Molly's should make dairy-free ice cream, and I think it's a great idea. What do you think?

That's smart! Sierra responded. I bet lots of people would be glad it's on the menu.

Great idea! Allie replied. Let me talk to my mom.

"Allie said she'd talk to her mom," I told Kai. Then I leaned in. "So, you're not mad at me anymore?"

Kai frowned. "Ask me again when you've actually made it up to me," he said. "Layla still thinks I'm the brother of a super-rude sister."

"I promise I'll make it up to you!" I said. Then I got up to leave the kitchen.

"Oh yeah," Kai said. He paused for a moment. "I saw your blog post this morning. It was nice."

"It was true," I said. Then I left the room, smiling.

Kai was talking to me again! I knew I still had to work hard to make him forgive me, but I already felt so relieved. I was proud of myself for trying to make things better again.

*I'm the queen of—* I broke off my thought as the evil Queen of Hearts popped into my mind. Hadn't I learned my lesson? I couldn't be too "extra" and get carried away again.

*Good job, Tamiko!* I told myself, and that felt about right.

## CHAPTER TWELVE

# SWEET SURPRISES

The next morning my phone buzzed with a video chat request. It was early in the morning for a weekend, but I was already up and dressed for my cross-country meet. I answered it, and Allie and Sierra popped up on the screen.

"My mom wants to know if we can meet her in the industrial kitchen before the shop opens tomorrow," Allie said. "She loves the idea of dairy-free ice cream and wants us to test out some new flavors. Actually, she said she had already been experimenting with vegan-friendly options, and dairy-free ice cream would appeal to people who don't eat dairy for all kinds of reasons."

"Kai was right! This is a good business move," I said.

"I've already been researching flavors," Sierra said. "I was thinking coconut milk might go really well with pineapple. We could do a tropical flavor!"

"Send me your ideas, and I'll send them to Mom," Allie said. "That way she can pick up ingredients before we meet."

"I might not have time to research," I said. "I have cross-country, and then I have—a thing." I avoided mentioning my study session with Ewan. My friends wouldn't understand that it wasn't a date.

"No problem," Allie said. "Can you both be there around nine thirty?"

"I'd wake up at dawn to make this thing right with Layla," I said.

"Nine thirty's not a problem," Sierra said.

"Great!" Allie said. "Then I'll see you tomorrow."

"What are you doing today, Alley Cat?" I asked.

"Not much," she said. "Some homework. And I have a thing this afternoon too."

I almost asked what her "thing" was, but I swallowed my curiosity just in time. I didn't want Allie asking the same question right back to me.

After my cross-country meet (I beat my best time by more than a minute, but I came in twelfth because our competition was really tough), I showered and got dressed for my study "thing" with Ewan. After searching online for "casual study outfits for teens" for thirty minutes, I decided on a T-shirt I'd gotten in Tokyo, with skinny jeans and my denim jacket.

Mom had already agreed to drive me to the library. The conversation had gone something like this.

"Sure, I'll drive you. Who are you studying with?"

"Just a kid from my class."

"Which kid?"

"Ewan Kim."

Mom raised an eyebrow. "Ewan, who sketched your portrait for an art class? And you had to sketch him?"

"Yup."

"Ewan Kim," Mom repeated.

"Yes," I said. "Is there a problem?"

Mom shook her head. "Nope. No problem at all," she replied. But she was grinning the whole time she drove me to the library, which was annoying because I was just studying with Ewan. I knew she thought it was some kind of date or something. Which it wasn't. A date is when two people go do something fun together.

"Tamiko, don't leave the library without letting me know," she said. "I'll come get you in an hour. Got it?"

"Got it," I said, and I bounded up the library steps.

The library was a huge building on the beach side of town. It was even bigger than the town hall. I headed to the Study Center, a room with glass walls where you could have quiet conversations as long as you spoke softly. Inside I found one girl studying by herself, a tutor helping a little boy with math, and Ewan.

"Hi, Tamiko," he whispered.

"Hey," I said, and sat down across the table from him. Then neither of us said anything for a few seconds. It was a teensy bit awkward.

"So, um, do you want to focus more on vocabulary or conjugating verbs?" I asked him.

"Verbs, I think," Ewan replied.

"Me too," I said. I reached for my backpack. "I brought the worksheet that Señora Hernandez gave us for the last test. I figured out where I went wrong. I thought we could go over it."

"Sure," he said, and then he looked behind me. "Hey, isn't that your friend Allie?"

I turned my head. There, standing in one of the book aisles, was Allie. She had a book in her hands, and a boy with dark hair was leaning over her shoulder, looking at it. It was Colin, the boy she had a crush on!

I guess her "thing" was the same as my "thing"!

Allie must have sensed me looking at her, because she turned her head and looked right at me. We stared at each other, wide-eyed, for a second. Finally I waved, and she waved back. Then she turned back to Colin, and I turned back to Ewan.

"So, uh, where were we?" I asked.

"Conjugating verbs," he said, and we launched into the study session. But in the back of my mind, I wondered how bad Allie's teasing would be when I saw her the next morning. She and Sierra loved to tease me about Ewan!

But truth be told, there was really nothing to tease me about. Ewan and I studied for about an hour. Then Ewan looked at his phone.

"Well, um, I guess I have to get home," he said. "Thanks, Tamiko."

"You mean '*gracias*,' right?" I said.

He grinned. *"Sí, gracias."*

And then he left, and that was that. Just your ordinary, non-romantic study session. And that's exactly what I would say to Allie if she teased me about it!

"Tamiko, how did you do in your cross-country meet yesterday?" Mrs. S. asked me when I walked into the industrial kitchen the next morning.

"Twelfth place," I replied. "But I beat my personal record."

"That's great, Tamiko!" she said. "Come on in, wash up, and put on some gloves and a hair protector, please."

Allie came in from the other room, carrying a metal tray with ingredients on it. She looked like a mushroom with the puffy hair cap on, but I didn't laugh. I knew I was going to look just like her soon.

"How is Sierra going to stuff all her hair into this?" I wondered, stretching the thin elastic band of the plastic cap.

"These hair caps are pretty stretchy," Mrs. S. replied. "I hope you don't mind doing it. The regulations for making food here are even more strict than the serving guidelines we follow at the shop."

The industrial kitchen was in a small, concrete

building at the edge of Bayville, away from the beach. According to Allie, it was run by a nonprofit community group, and anybody who had a food business could rent the space. Apparently, you couldn't just make food in your kitchen and sell it. There were all kinds of rules about things like handwashing stations and keeping food at certain temperatures. Also, the industrial kitchen had bigger and better equipment than a regular kitchen—extra-large ovens for cooking big batches of things at the same time, for example. A large walk-in freezer. And also, a commercial ice cream machine.

Sierra rushed in, breathless. "Am I late?" she asked. "And why is everyone wearing weird hats?"

"You're right on time," Mrs. S. said.

I handed her gloves and a hair protector. "Wash up and put these on," I instructed. Sierra's hair was so long and heavy that she turned into an extra-large mushroom. Soon we were all ready.

"I did a little bit of experimenting with vegan ice cream," Mrs. S. began, "and I think cream of coconut comes closest to tasting like real ice cream. Here's a sample of a basic vanilla."

We used tiny plastic tasting spoons to get a taste of

the vanilla dairy-free ice cream from a paper carton. It felt smooth and creamy in my mouth.

"Yummy," Sierra said.

"I can taste the coconut, but not in a bad way," I said.

Allie nodded. "It takes a back seat to the vanilla."

"I'm going to experiment using the coconut base to make a chocolate fudge flavor," her mom said. "In the meantime, I'd like you to taste the vanilla along with some of the ingredients we have here, and see which ones you like best."

She pointed to the tray that Allie had been carrying. There were little bowls that Allie had carefully labeled. I spotted crushed macadamia nuts, chai syrup, chopped strawberries, chopped pineapple, and more.

"How should we do this?" Sierra asked.

"I'm going to put some of the coconut base on my spoon, top it with one of these, and see how the two taste together," Allie said. She pulled a small notebook out of her back pocket. "If we do the flavors at the same time, I can take notes."

"That's a great idea," I said. "How about we start with strawberry?"

We all tasted the ice cream base with the strawberry.

"It goes together," I said.

"It does," Allie agreed. "But it's not . . . luxurious."

Sierra laughed. "Luxurious! I never thought ice cream could be luxurious. I thought only cars and mansions and jewels could be."

"Well, I think our dairy-free ice cream needs to taste the same way," Allie said. "Rich. Special."

"I know what Allie means," I said. "It could be more . . . decadent."

Allie jotted in her notebook, and we moved on to the next flavor.

Now, as much as I didn't want to be teased about Ewan, I couldn't resist the chance to ask Allie about Colin.

"So, Allie, did you find anything *interesting* in the library yesterday?" I asked her.

"Not really," Allie said, looking me in the eye. "How about you?"

"Nothing," I said.

Sierra looked at both of us. "Is 'library' code for something? You guys are acting weird."

Allie didn't answer her. "Speaking of libraries, I

realized that I've actually met Layla before. I thought she looked familiar, but I couldn't figure out why. Then I remembered that we were on the same volunteer schedule at the library."

"Wow, really?" I asked. Allie volunteered at the library by reading books to little kids.

Allie nodded. "She must have switched days, because I haven't seen her in a while," she said. "But I remember her because all the little kids loved her. One day these two kids were arguing over a book about sharks. They almost tore the book in half! But Layla calmed them down really quickly. She found another book about sharks and got them to take turns. I was really impressed."

"I probably would have taken the book from them and thrown it out the window," I said, and I wasn't exactly joking. I could get pretty impatient with the fussy customers at Molly's.

"Layla sounds like a very cool person," Sierra said.

"For sure," I said glumly. "Which makes me feel even worse for being a jerk to her!"

"Don't beat yourself up, Tamiko," Sierra said. "This dairy-free ice cream idea is a nice gesture."

"So how does everybody like the chai flavor?"

Allie asked pointedly, putting us back on track.

"It's really cozy and nice," I said. "And it's a complement to our other fall flavors."

"Good point!" Allie said, writing that down.

A short while later we had tested all the flavors. Mrs. S. appeared with a metal bowl of the chocolate fudge.

"Try the fudge," she said. "And then let me know what you think of the flavor mix-ins."

"Mmmmmmmmm!" Sierra said. "This is, like, everything you want real ice cream to be. I think you nailed it, Mrs. S."

"I agree," I said. "It's luxurious!"

"Hey, that's *my* word," Allie said. "But I think you need to put this on the menu. Everybody loves chocolate. This would be a hit."

"What about the other flavors?" Mrs. S. asked.

Allie looked through the notes. "Strawberry was a little basic. Pineapple was nice and bright. The macadamia nuts needed something—like chocolate chips, maybe. The butterscotch was too sweet. The chai was cozy and fall-like."

"Hmm. Maybe I'll do two flavors, the chocolate fudge and the chai," Allie's mom said. "And then we can come up with some new dairy-free flavors for the holidays."

"That's perfect!" I said. "I can blitz social media with an announcement. When do you think you'll put them in the shop?"

"I think I can do it by next week," she replied. She looked at the clock on the wall. "Let's clean up here and get over to Molly's. There's a craft fair on the pavilion today, and I think we're going to get a lot of foot traffic."

"Will do," I said. "But first, some pictures."

I snapped a few shots of the ice cream flavors. They weren't glamorous enough for social media, but just right for what I needed them for.

On the ride to the shop, I texted my brother with the photos.

Two new dairy-free flavors coming to Molly's next week, I typed. Please bring Layla! The cups are on me.

Thanks, Kai texted back, but he didn't say anything else.

I leaned back in my seat. *This has to work*, I thought. *If I can't make this up to Kai and Layla, I'll be forever known as the queen of mean!*

## CHAPTER THIRTEEN

# A FABULOUS FALL AFTER ALL

I got to Molly's early the next Sunday to begin the dairy-free social media blitz. I'd wanted to do it a few days in advance, but Mrs. S. had worked all week to perfect the flavors, and she'd wanted me to wait until she was sure she was going to serve them. I'd crossed my fingers that she would, because I didn't want to disappoint Layla if she came.

But in the morning, Mrs. S. had texted me to say: We're on! I got to the shop as soon as I could. Allie was already there with her mom, and she had a perfectly scooped bowl of each flavor waiting for me in the freezer.

"What do you think?" she asked, placing the bowls

on the counter. "Are they photo ready, or should we dress them up a little bit?"

I thought for a moment. "The chocolate fudge could use a cherry," I said. "And maybe, for the chai . . . butterscotch chips?"

"That would look nice," Allie agreed. "Let me check first to make sure they're dairy-free."

She disappeared into the back room and then came out. "Butterscotch chips are good!"

We added the toppings, and then I looked for the best backdrop. I decided to use the window sign I'd made that read: NOW SERVING DELICIOUS DAIRY-FREE ICE CREAM! LACTOSE-FREE AND VEGAN! I propped it up against the napkin holder on one of the tables and arranged the two perfect bowls of ice cream in front of it. Then I snapped a bunch of photos.

I chose the best photo and uploaded it to the Molly's SuperSnap page.

"BRAND NEW AT MOLLY'S! Come on down today to try our two new dairy-free flavors: Luxurious Chocolate Fudge and Fall Fabulous Chai Spice. #MollysIceCream #Bayville #Vegan #DairyFree #LactoseFree #DairyFreeDessert."

Then I shared the post on the Bayville community page and my personal page.

"The word is out," I said. "This is going to be great! Let me get the signs up."

I walked over to the window. The *Bayville Monthly* cover was hanging in the best spot, and I left it up. But I took down the sign congratulating me and replaced it with one of the dairy-free signs. Then I posted a dairy-free sign on the ice cream freezer, too, in case people missed it outside.

Sierra walked in looking worried. "Wait, I can't be late! I gave myself plenty of time this morning."

"You're not," I said. "I just wanted to get Operation Layla started."

Sierra frowned. "Operation Layla? You're not meddling in your brother's business again, are you?"

"Relax," I told her. "I'm not meddling this time. I don't know if Kai will come, but I offered to treat Layla and him to the new dairy-free ice cream. I just want to apologize."

Sierra nodded. "That's a good plan," she said. "I hope they come."

"Incoming!" Allie said, and our first customers of the day walked through the door: two high school girls.

"Welcome to Molly's!" I said. "Can I interest you in some of our brand-new, decadently delicious dairy-free ice cream today?"

One of the girls frowned. "Is all the ice cream dairy-free?"

"No," I replied. "We're just introducing two new flavors."

"Can we still get regular ice cream?" the other girl asked.

"Of course," I said.

"Then I'll have a vanilla cup with rainbow sprinkles," she replied, and her friend ordered the same. After I served them, Allie came up to me.

"Maybe don't push the dairy-free ice cream," she whispered. "If people want it, they'll ask for it."

I bit my lip. I knew that sometimes people didn't read signs. Half of them asked "What flavors do you have?" when the giant flavor board was right up on the wall. And I really wanted the dairy-free ice cream to be a success! But I didn't want to upset Allie either.

"Got it," I said, and then more customers came in.

We took fourteen orders of regular ice cream after that, and nobody asked for dairy-free.

"Welcome to Molly's! Can I interest you in one

of our fabulous fall flavors? We've got Pumpkin Caramel Swirl, Maple Butter Pecan, Apple Pie, and dairy-free Fall Fabulous Chai Spice."

I tried that for the next five customers, and still nobody wanted the dairy-free.

Then a middle-aged man with salt-and-pepper hair came in and looked at the sign on the ice cream freezer.

"So it's true? You have dairy-free ice cream?" he asked before I could greet him.

"We sure do," I replied. "Luxurious Chocolate Fudge and Fall Fabulous Chai Spice."

"I saw your post, and I couldn't believe it," he said. "I love ice cream, and usually I get a kiddie-size cup and suffer, but it's worth it. Now I can't wait to try the dairy-free. I'll have the Luxurious Chocolate Fudge, please."

"You got it," I said, and Allie scooped it up. I added some chocolate sprinkles, since Mrs. S. had already assured me that they were dairy-free. "Here's your sprinkle of happy. Enjoy!"

It made me feel great to see how happy the customer was! He came back up to the counter on his way out.

"That was delicious!" he said. "Please keep this on the menu. I'll be back!"

I looked over at Allie.

"I heard him," Allie said, grinning.

About twenty minutes after that, a group of teen-age girls came in, and I repeated my pitch.

"Pumpkin Caramel Swirl, Maple Butter Pecan, Apple Pie, and two new dairy-free flavors," I said.

One of the girls turned to her friend. "See, Violet? I *told* you they had vegan ice cream."

Violet looked at me skeptically. "Is it really vegan? No animal products at all?"

"Right. Our dairy-free flavors are also vegan," I said. "What flavor would you like? Chocolate fudge or chai?"

"Chai, please," Violet said. "In a cup."

Allie scooped it out, and I added the sprinkles. "Here's your vegan sprinkle of happy," I said, and Violet actually smiled.

I looked at the clock on the wall. It was almost two o'clock, and still no sign of Kai. What if Layla had refused to come? That made me nervous, but I pushed the thought away and took care of the next customers.

"May I taste the dairy-free?" the woman asked.

"Sure," I said, and I handed her a tiny tasting spoon of the chocolate fudge.

She tasted it and nodded. "This is just as creamy and delicious as your other flavors," she said. "What's it made of?"

"There's a coconut milk base," I told her.

"Very nice," she said. "I'm going to get some Maple Butter Pecan today, but I'd love to take home a pint of the dairy-free. I've got guests coming over next weekend, and I think they'll appreciate this."

"You got it," I said, and I started to relax a little bit. People weren't clamoring for the dairy-free ice cream, but I had a feeling it was doing well enough to stay on the menu.

I was right. Over the next two hours we sold a decent amount of both the chocolate fudge and the chai. That would have made me happy, but my shift was almost over, and there was still no sign of Kai.

"Well, I guess I blew it," I told Allie and Sierra. "Layla is never going to forgive me."

"Don't be so sure," Sierra said, looking out the window.

Kai and Layla walked through the door. I practically ran out from behind the counter.

"Layla, I just want to say I'm SO SORRY about the other day," I said.

"It's okay," Layla said. "Thanks for the apology."

Phew. I couldn't believe Layla actually forgave me! "To make it up to you, I want to treat you and Kai to some dairy-free ice cream," I said.

"Thanks," Layla said. "Kai said Molly's just started making it."

"Yeah, well, it was his idea," I answered. "He wanted you to be able to try Molly's Ice Cream."

Layla looked at Kai, surprised. "You did that just for me?" she asked.

Kai blushed. "Yeah," he said. "I mean, it's for all the other lactose intolerant people too. And I didn't actually make the ice cream. Mrs. Shear did. . . ."

"That was so thoughtful, Kai! Thank you!" Layla said, smiling at him. My brother turned so red that even Allie, Sierra, and I could feel his awkwardness. Allie turned bright red in sympathy with him!

I returned to my spot behind the counter. "We have dairy-free chocolate fudge and chai spice," I said. "The cups are on me."

"Then I'll take a chocolate fudge cup, please," Layla replied.

"And I'll take a chai one," Kai said.

*Smart thinking, Brother!* I thought. He could have

had any flavor, but he chose a dairy-free one in soli-darity with Layla. When I handed over the cones, Kai smiled at me, and he didn't even have to say anything for me to know that he wasn't mad anymore.

Kai and Layla took their cones to a corner table. They talked and ate, and seemed to be having a good time. I tried not to stare at them, but I was so curious! And they looked so cute together. And they stayed and talked for a while even after they'd finished their ice cream.

Kai and Layla both waved when they left. I felt like a giant weight had been lifted off my shoulders. Layla had forgiven me! Kai looked happy! With this mistake behind me, I could focus on having a fabu-lous fall after all.

Sierra came over to me as we were finishing up our shift. "It's a good sign that they stayed and talked," she said. "I think Layla really likes him."

"I hope so!" I said. "Kai deserves to be happy. And also, I am tired of quiet, mopey Kai!"

"You know, Tamiko, we should have gotten a photo of Kai and Layla holding their ice cream," Allie said. "To show people actually eating the dairy-free and smiling and enjoying it."

I nodded. "That would have been great! But I can take a shot of you and Sierra eating it instead. You both have spectacular smiles."

"Yes, we do," Sierra agreed. I scooped one perfect chocolate fudge cone and one perfect chai cone. Then I handed one to each of my friends and gazed around the shop.

"Natural light is best," I said, checking to see where the sun was coming in. "Why don't you two stand in front of the ice cream counter?"

Allie and Sierra obeyed, but they were both facing forward, and the picture looked a little stiff.

"How about you face each other," I said, peering at the shots on my phone. "Now start to lick the cones, but turn your faces toward me. Just your face, not your body, Allie. Good."

I took a shot that was a close-up of their heads, and then I backed up to get a full-body shot of both of them.

"Hold that pose," I said, and took another step back.

"Tamiko, be careful!" Allie cried.

I banged into the table behind me, knocking over the napkin dispenser. I caught it as it slid off the table, right before it could hit the floor.

"Are you okay?" Sierra asked as she and Allie ran over to me.

"I'm okay! I'm okay! I'll be more careful next time," I promised.

That was Sierra and Allie. Always looking out for me. Always there to let me know when I wasn't being careful—with napkin dispensers, or with other people's feelings. I grinned at them.

"And when I'm not being careful enough, I'm glad I've got friends who are always watching my back," I said.

"Aww. Tamiko, that's so unlike you to say!" Sierra said.

I put my hands on my hips and rolled my eyes dramatically. "I mean, I *guess* you girls are okay," I said haughtily. Then I laughed. "Better?"

"That's more like it!" Allie giggled.

"Seriously, though," I said. "I'll always be kind of extra, but thanks for keeping it in check."

"*No hay problema, chica*," Sierra said. Allie pulled us in for a group hug—well, a sort-of hug. They both held their ice cream cones out to the sides to keep them out of our hug.

"Sprinkle Sundays sisters forever!" I cheered.

### DON'T MISS BOOK 12:
## ICE CREAM AND SWEET DREAMS

It was one of those first really cold days of fall that make you excited for winter and turtleneck sweaters and hot chocolate. I stared out the window of Molly's Ice Cream Shop, where I was working my regular Sunday shift with my two best friends, Allie Shear and Tamiko Sato, and pictured myself pulling my favorite sunny yellow sweater out of storage and putting on fuzzy socks when I got home later.

Our town of Bayville was a beachside town, which meant that usually we had a steady stream of ice cream lovers coming through the shop. But on days like today, when the thermometer dipped below

45 degrees and the wind was blowing, people had their minds on other things.

"Earth to Sierra, are you in there?" Allie teased, waving a hand in front of my face.

"She's probably writing song lyrics in her head," said Tamiko, who was holding chalk and an eraser, and staring up at the shop's two giant chalkboards. One was for the daily special, something our social marketing and flavor genius Tamiko was excellent at dreaming up, and one was for Allie's ice cream and book pairings, where our bookworm Allie appealed to the book lovers in town by matching a classic read with just the right treat.

But today both boards had been wiped bare, and Tamiko stood staring at the wall, as if she didn't have a single idea.

"No lyrics in this head!" I replied. "At least, not today. Anyway, Tessa writes most of our song lyrics. She's the one with all the inspiration."

Tessa was one of my bandmates in my rock band, the Wildflowers. And while we did write and perform our own music, I was the lead singer, and mostly only helped with the composition of our songs, not the lyrics.

"Maybe you should call her," Tamiko suggested. "Because, girl—we need some inspiration *here*. *Now*. This place is dead! We need an amazing, fresh fall flavor to bring people in."

"I agree," said Allie. "We have a reputation for more than just delicious homemade ice cream. It's our originality that keeps people coming back."

Tamiko sighed. "I tried to liven things up after my trip to Japan this summer by introducing some of their most interesting soft cream flavors, like miso, black sesame, and soybean flour. I don't know why it didn't work!"

Allie and I looked at each other and laughed.

"Even my mom couldn't make soybean flour ice cream tempting enough to sell well," said Allie. "And she can make anything work! Look how well all of the new lactose-free flavors have done."

Thanks to some recent "inspiration" from Tamiko's brother, Kai, Molly's had also started carrying one or two lactose-free flavors. I couldn't believe how good they were—and made entirely with coconut milk!

"So then *where* can we go for inspiration around here?" Tamiko wondered aloud.

"We went to the boardwalk a few times," Allie

replied. "It was fun, but it didn't help us much."

"Maybe you should call Colin and ask him for ideas," I said, nudging Allie with my shoulder.

Allie had recently been spending a lot of time studying at the library with Colin, her longtime crush and closest friend at Vista Green Middle School.

"Why would I ask Colin?" Allie asked, blushing furiously and wiping at an imaginary spot on the clean countertops. "I doubt he knows anything about ice cream flavors."

Just then Allie's mother appeared from the little office at the back of the shop, which we all called "backstage."

"It's awfully quiet out here, girls. What's going on? No crazy new flavor ideas, Tamiko? No book pairings, Allie? Sierra can't pour on her charm with no customers in here!"

I loved when Mrs. Shear said I was charming. It wasn't something I did consciously, I just happened to have a very outgoing personality and really like people. When I was around a crowd, I lit up and felt naturally cheerful. What can I say? I'm a people person, and proud of it!

"No new pairings or specials yet," Allie said. "It's

cold outside and our brains are tired from all of our homework and eighth-grade responsibilities. We need something exciting to get our creative juices flowing!"

Mrs. Shear pulled something from her back pocket and laid it down on the counter in front of us. It was a brochure for Peg and Mary's Ice Cream Museum and Factory Tour.

"An ice cream *museum*?" Tamiko squealed. "How have I never heard of this before?"

"It sounds amazing!" I said. "Can you imagine the toppings they must have? And different types of cones?"

"And all the old equipment and hand cranks?" Allie added.

Mrs. Shear beamed. "I thought you girls would be interested. What do you think about the Sprinkle Sundays sisters going on a little 'research' field trip with me next week? Maybe on Tuesday? I can check with your parents and make sure it's okay."

We didn't waste a second. All three of us screamed at once, "Yes!"

The only thing more fun than a field trip with your two best friends, was a field trip to an *ice cream factory* with your two best friends.

"Do they have samples?" Allie asked. "They must have *samples*, right?"

Mrs. Shear nodded. "Oh yes, indeed. They have a movie about the old days of making ice cream, a production room, a 'Flavoroom,' and even a flavor graveyard for flavors that are no longer . . . er, living. I think this is just the thing we need to gear up for fall and winter! When you have a year-round business based on a summer staple, you need to always be prepared to think big. Now, girls, put some music on, brainstorm, and see what you can come up with for today!"

Mrs. Shear left the brochure for us to look at and went backstage again to deal with whatever office work had piled up.

Tamiko browsed the brochure, while I put on an upbeat song from my current favorite playlist on my phone.

Allie stared and stared at the chalkboard before finally saying, "What do you guys think of pairing *Alice's Adventures in Wonderland* by Lewis Carroll with our Tea and Crumpets flavor? After all, the Mad Hatter tea party scene is pretty famous, and tea is a good drink for a fall day. . . ."

"I love it!" I said, clapping my hands. Allie always came up with the best ideas for book pairings.

Tamiko shook her head sadly. "You're doing your job, Alley Cat. If only I could do mine. My mind has just been blank lately! I promise—I'm going to do better, or my name isn't Tamiko Sato!"

I wrapped my arm around Tamiko's shoulder and gave her a squeeze. "Knowing you, you'll have five fabulous new ideas before tomorrow. Don't worry—we're a team! And we've got our factory tour to look forward to. We'll get tons of new ideas!"

Tamiko nodded, but I could tell she still felt badly. Recently, Tamiko had gone through a bit of a braggy phase, thinking she was the queen of just about everything—art, schoolwork, our jobs at Molly's. She'd ended up hurting her brother in the process, and since then, she had been just a bit more subdued than usual. I was ready for the old outrageous and outlandish (but not braggy!) Tamiko to make her return.

"We're going to come up with something new and fabulous or we're not the Sprinkle Sundays sisters," I said. I wrapped my other arm around Allie and pulled them both to me. "Get ready for greatness!"

After work I walked home, enjoying the chill in the air and wondering what delicious food my Papi might be making for dinner. My parents were both veterinarians and ran their own veterinary clinic. They often worked long hours during the week, so they always made sure to have a big family dinner on Sunday evenings, and usually my father was the chef. Both of my parents had been born in Cuba, and my father liked nothing better than to spend an afternoon cooking up one of his grandmother's favorite recipes for the family.

I was feeling so excited about the crisp fall air and the ice cream museum field trip with my friends that I practically skipped up the steps to my front door.

When I burst inside, I dropped my bag in the hallway and yelled out that I was home.

*"Hola! Estoy en casa!"*

From upstairs, my mother replied, *"Hola*, Sierra!" but from the kitchen I heard only a "Whoops! That was more than a pinch."

A *pinch*? A pinch of what?

I smelled something rich and slightly smoky cooking. I couldn't quite place it, which was unusual because my nose knew most of my father's signature dishes by heart. I headed toward the kitchen, pausing to pet my cat, Marshmallow, as he twined between my legs.

"What is that yummy smell, Papi?" I asked as I stepped into the kitchen. But to my surprise, my father wasn't there. It was my twin, Isa, standing in front of the big gas range, stirring an enormous pot of something. "Oh, hey. What are you doing?"

Isa flipped her bangs out of her face and rolled her eyes. She was practically an expert at both gestures. "I'm making *cocido de garbanzos*—chickpea stew."

I thought hard for a moment. I didn't remember ever having *cocido de garbanzos* before. "Is that one of Papi's dishes?"

Isa shook her head. "No. He got called in for an emergency—a Schnauzer ate some raisins and needed his stomach pumped—and Mami is catching up on paperwork, so he told me I could be in charge of dinner. So I went online, found a recipe, and went for it. I think I just overdid it on the paprika, though."

Isa shrugged, as if it didn't matter too much one way or the other. I had *not* inherited the cooking bug from our father, and my idea of making a snack was to grab a granola bar on my way from one activity to another. But Isa, who was my identical twin and yet pretty much my opposite in every single way, had begun to cook recently and was trying increasingly harder dishes.

I couldn't help being impressed. I had almost zero confidence in my kitchen skills (I didn't even scoop the ice cream at Molly's—I ran the cash register and handled most of the customer service issues!), and would never have tried to make a completely new recipe by myself without my father there to help me.

Isa was always willing to try something hard and risk failing. That was why she was the only girl on an all-boys travel soccer team. She'd had the guts to show up and try out for it. And once they saw how good she was, they had to take her. It was something I'd always admired about her.

"Will Papi be home in time to eat with us?" I asked.

Isa shook her head. "I don't think so. It's ready now, and he said not to wait for him in case they have to keep the Schnauzer for observation for a few hours."

"How did the owners not know that raisins are poisonous to dogs?" I wondered aloud. "We've never even *had* a dog and we know that. Raisins, grapes, avocado, gum with xylitol, chocolate. They're all bad for dogs."

Isa laughed. "I know, right? But I guess everyone can't be the daughters of two veterinarians. We've grown up listening to all the things our parents have had to fix for other people's pets, so it makes sense that we'd know it."

Something about the way Isa had grouped us together, as "the daughters of two veterinarians," made me feel strangely warm inside. Normally Isa tried to pretend that we *weren't* identical twins. She wore black almost exclusively, while I wore bright colors, textured tights, and fun leggings. She'd had her hair cut into a fauxhawk a year ago, and dyed the tips purple, while I left mine long and curly and naturally brown. It was nice to hear her mention us being on the same team.

"Your stew sounds great," I told her. "It's the perfect thing to eat on this first really cold autumn day!"

Isa beamed, clearly pleased by my compliment. "That's exactly why I picked it," she said. "Cold weather means soup!"

"I'll set the table," I offered, "since you did all the cooking. And I'll tell Mami to come and eat with us."

The stew turned out to be delicious, and while our Sunday dinner wasn't as festive as it usually was with my dad gone, it was still pretty nice. I felt grateful, and for a moment, felt a pang for my friend Allie, whose parents had divorced over a year ago. She now split her time between her mom's house and her dad's apartment. She'd even had to transfer schools at the start of seventh grade, which meant that she no longer was at school with Tamiko and me. Her parents did a great job of keeping things friendly, and they even had dinner together, all four of them, sometimes. But I wondered what it would be like in my house to not have our regular Sunday family dinners.

It left me with a decidedly kind and gooey feeling in my stomach. So much so that I volunteered to do all the dishes myself, even though I absolutely hated cleaning up. My parents did too, which was why our house was usually a bit, well, untidy. But I did the dishes anyway, so that Mami could get back to her paperwork and because Isa had obviously worked hard to make our dinner. She cheered when I offered and practically ran to escape up to her room.

By the time I'd finished the dishes and had wiped all the counters, I was enjoying the lingering warmth and smell of the kitchen so much that I decided to do my homework there, even though I normally preferred the privacy of my bedroom.

I wanted to make sure I saw Papi when he got home, and I wanted to also remind myself how lucky I was to have my family together, all in one house. Maybe we weren't perfect all the time, but we were there for each other.

I gathered my books and spread out at the kitchen table. I started on my geometry homework first. Even though I was usually a whiz at math, geometry was taking some time for me to get used to. Rays, planes, complementary and supplementary angles . . . it was like a new language. I loved computing numbers in my head, and in fact, did it all the time working the register at Molly's. But geometry was different. It was about rules.

To my surprise, after I'd been working for about a half an hour, Isa came back downstairs and plopped down in the chair across from me.

She was nibbling on a dark chocolate bar. It must have been stashed up in her room. If Isa had a weakness, it was dark chocolate.

She sat quietly for a minute or two, just watching me work on problem number fifteen.

This was not how things normally went in our house. Isa did not *linger* around any of us—she liked to be alone. Something had to be up.

"What's up?" I said finally.

She shrugged innocently. "Why should something be up?" she asked.

I gave her the I-know-my-twin-sister face and raised an eyebrow. "Since when do you enjoy watching me try to figure out an angle?"

"It's 37 degrees," she said. "You've got to subtract 53 from 90, because *that* one is a right angle, you can tell by the little mark there, and that's how you know they total 90. Ta-da!" Then she grinned at me.

I looked back down at my paper and saw that she was right. I hurriedly did the equation on my homework sheet so that my teacher could see how I got the answer.

"Thanks," I said.

"No big deal." Another minute or two passed, and then Isa said, "So, what's new with you, Rock Star? Do the Wildflowers have any gigs coming up? I haven't heard you practicing as much."

This conversation was almost unprecedented. Isa cared about my *band*? She had come to a few of our performances, but she almost never asked me—randomly—how things were going with the group.

"Um, well, we've been practicing, but I guess not quite as much since school started. Everyone's had so much schoolwork. Plus, we don't have a gig coming up right now. But I'm sure we'll get back in our groove as everyone settles into the school year."

"Would you say your voice is in good shape?" she prodded.

I put my pencil down hard. "Excuse me, *what*? Why are you asking me all this stuff?"

Isa opened her eyes wide, playing the innocent.

"Can't I take an interest in my dear, sweet, twin sister?"

I narrowed my own eyes. Something was up. Something was *definitely* up. "Spill it, Isa. You're acting weird, maybe even more weird than when you snuck a *snake* into the house last year and told me your grand plan to hide it from Mami and Papi was to keep it in your closet forever."

Isa laughed. "Not one of my best ideas."

I laughed too, in spite of myself. I couldn't help it. Seeing Isa happy made me happy. "Just tell me whatever is going on with you, so I can finish my homework."

"Okay, okay." She pulled a folded piece of paper from the front pocket of her hoodie and handed it to me. The paper felt soft, the creases slightly worn, as if it had been folded and unfolded many times.

I opened it. It was an ad.

It's time to find the
NEXT YOUNG SINGING
SENSATION!
Could it be YOU?
Come and audition for the

**WHO'S A STAR?** singing contest!
If you're selected as a finalist, you will
appear on our local TV station,
where fans will decide our big winner!

"What do you think?" said Isa. "I saw the flyer posted on the bulletin board outside the grocery store earlier and I thought you should do it."

I felt a series of tingles all over my body. I was nervous, excited, scared, hopeful, and anxious. A singing contest? It was like a dream come true!

"When is it?" I asked, my eyes scanning the tiny type at the bottom of the page.

"It's the end of next week."

"Next *week*? Isa, I can't be ready by then. What will I sing? Am I even good enough to try out?"

Isa raised her eyebrows. "There's only one way to find out, right?"

I nodded. I could feel something like hope blooming in my stomach. I knew I couldn't do it by myself, though—I'd need my band to help prepare me. And of course I needed Allie and Tamiko to tell me I could even do it!

I wanted to call them all immediately. But I also

wanted to tell them in person. And maybe think about it overnight . . . just in case. Just in case I wasn't sure I was brave enough to audition in front of real talent professionals and other kids who'd been singing much longer than I had. After all, I'd just started with my band last year. I hadn't even had any formal training or anything!

I was sunny Sierra. I was charming and outgoing. I was good at juggling lots of things and tried to be a good friend to my Sprinkle Sundays sisters.

But was I a star? I didn't know. Then again, it seemed like there was a way to find out.

Looking for another great book?
Find it
**IN THE MIDDLE**.

Fun, fantastic books for kids
in the in-be**TWEEN** age.

IntheMiddleBooks.com

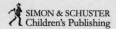

# Still Hungry?

## There's always room for a Cupcake!

CUPCAKE DIARIES

Emma all stirred up!

by coco simon

CUPCAKE DIARIES

Alexis cool as a cupcake

by coco simon

Katie and the cupcake war

CUPCAKE DIARIES

by coco simon

CUPCAKE DIARIES

Mia's boiling point

Emma, smile and say "cupcake!"

CUPCAKE DIARIES

Alexis gets frosted

CUPCAKE DIARIES

by coco simon

CUPCAKE DIARIES

Katie's new recipe

Mia a matter of taste

CUPCAKE DIARIES

Emma sugar and spice and everything nice

CUPCAKE DIARIES

CUPCAKE DIARIES

Alexis and the missing ingredient

by coco simon

Katie sprinkles surprises

CUPCAKE DIARIES

Mia fashion plates and cupcakes

CUPCAKE DIARIES

# sewZoey

Zoey's clothing design blog puts her on the A-list in the fashion world . . . but when it comes to school, will she be teased, or will she be a trendsetter? Find out in the Sew Zoey series: